I0630684

THE CREW

MIKE RYAN

MIKERYANBOOKS.COM

J ack and Stacy Carter were near the end of their rope. They both had steady jobs, though Stacy's was only part-time, but with two young children, they were barely making ends meet. Between the mortgage on their small house, car payments, insurance, bills, food, baby supplies, and all the little things that added up, there just wasn't anything left over. Some weeks they had to sacrifice paying one bill for another, alternating so that the same bill wasn't continuously late..

They'd been together for five years but had known each other for eight. Jack had a troubled youth, getting into trouble constantly until he was in his early twenties. He'd gotten mixed up with the wrong people, which he was totally honest about with Stacy, though she wouldn't agree to date him until he put all that in the past. It took him a few years to wise up, but eventually, he did, and left his criminal friends behind.

After bouncing around from job to job, Jack eventually hooked up with a construction company. It was long, hard hours, and he wasn't getting rich from it, but at least it was something. Stacy only worked part-time as a receptionist at a doctor's office. They couldn't afford daycare for the kids, and neither had family in the area who could watch them while they were at work during the day, so Stacy only worked ten to twenty hours a week, the two nights that the doctor had later hours, and on Saturdays when Jack was around to watch the kids.

With two children under the age of two, Jackson, who was about to turn two in another month, and Steven, who was only six months, Jack and Stacy were growing very frustrated with their current living situation. It seemed like every month they were worse off than the month before. They'd even begun arguing more often, which they hardly ever did before. Neither one was an argumentative person, but their lack of money was an ever-growing sore spot.

Jack had just gotten home from work, and it didn't take long for him and his wife to start going at it.

"We're running out of diapers," Stacy said. "We're gonna need more for tomorrow."

Jack sighed.

"We also need to go grocery shopping. There's not much left in the fridge," she continued.

Jack sighed again, throwing his arms up. "What do you want me to do? You know I don't get paid 'till Friday. We only have like fifty dollars in the bank, and we need some of that for gas."

"We might need formula too."

Jack rolled his eyes. "Is there anything else?" he asked sarcastically.

"Hey, don't have that attitude with me. It's not my fault we need things."

Jack immediately felt bad. "I know. I'm sorry."

"I sent out a couple feelers for other jobs that I can work at night. Hopefully one of them will work out."

"Then I'll be gone during the day, you'll be gone at night, we'll never see each other."

Stacy shrugged. "I mean, it's the only thing we can do right now."

"I'll figure something out."

Stacy looked at him, then into the living room at the kids, not really wanting to say what she was thinking. Her parents lived a couple hours away, moving farther away a couple of years ago to be closer to the beach. Jack didn't want to ask them for help as he knew they disapproved of him anyway, and he didn't want them to think he was a failure for not being able to take care of their daughter and his own family.

"I also thought about taking the kids to see my parents for a few weeks."

"A few weeks?!" Jack asked.

Stacy opened her mouth to talk, but no words

came out. She just stood there, trying to think of the best way to say it. "It's not fair to these kids, Jack. We barely have enough food. We run out of diapers constantly. How long do we keep up this charade that we don't need help? I mean, at least if we're there, I know they'll be clothed and fed. Right now, that's my only concern."

"What are you saying? Divorce?"

"No," Stacy said, wiping the tears from her eyes. "They've been wanting to see the kids. And if take them there for a few weeks and just let them know we're struggling, they'll be willing to help. I'm only thinking about the kids right now."

As much as Jack wanted to outright forbid the idea, he looked over at his children and had to at least entertain the notion. He then turned his attention back to his wife. "Let's just give it another week or two. At least wait and see if any of those jobs get back to you."

"And if they don't?"

"We'll figure it out at that time. Please?"

"You really think a week is going to make that much of a difference?" Stacy asked.

"Just let me see what else I can come up with, OK?"

"Do you have something else going on you haven't told me about?"

"No, but just give me a week, OK? Deal?"

"OK. One more week." Stacy reluctantly agreed, but something was gnawing at her, that her husband might be leaning towards going back to his old ways.

"You're not planning on doing something stupid, are you?"

"What? No."

"Because if you are, the kids need a father. Remember that."

DOMINIC PULLED into the driveway of the large estate, a three thousand square foot home, complete with all the upscale finishings and upgrades that one would expect of a home in that neighborhood. Every house in the area had expensive looking kitchens, full finished basements that housed game and theater rooms, in-ground pools, and nothing sold in the development for under a million dollars.

Dominic Cirella was a career criminal. Now in his late thirties, he was always looking for his next big score. Unlike some of his contemporaries, Cirella didn't bother with what he considered small-time jobs. He was only looking for big jobs with big money. If the job didn't pay at least a hundred thousand dollars, he wasn't interested, no matter how easy it might have been. After all, he was the leader of a four-man crew, so everything was split evenly. Plus, something was always given to Mark, the man who owned the house that Cirella just arrived at, since he was the one who usually set the jobs up.

Cirella's crew was a highly specialized and highly

effective unit. They were all friends, and they'd all
been with each other for close to fifteen years, except
for one. Danny Falk was the newest guy. He'd only
been with them for three years. He replaced Carter
when he left, though not immediately, as there was a
brief prison stretch for the rest of the team. Though
Falk was competent and effective, he never really fit in
with the others. They regarded him as a bit of a loose
cannon who had to be reeled in more often than not. If
he hadn't been as good as he was, the rest of the crew
would have discarded him long ago.

The team didn't like Falk as much as they liked
Carter, but he was good, so they put up with his
nonsense. Cirella, Isaac Brantly, and Noah Rollins had
all spent time in prison, effectively terminating the
team, causing Carter to go straight. Cirella spent three
years in the joint while Brantly and Rollins spent two
years each inside. Once they were all out, they
reformed the group. They initially had wanted Carter
to rejoin, but with Stacy now by his side, he had no
desire to go back to his old way of life. Though disappointed in being rebuffed, the team respected his decision and chose a new guy who came highly
recommended, and that person was Falk.

As Cirella walked along the concrete pathway to
the front of the house, Mark was already at the door
waiting for him. Mark was a middle-aged man in his
fifties. He was athletically built, had a full head of
mostly greying hair, and stood over six feet tall. He had

a family, wife, and two kids, though he never let them know his business. His wife knew he was mixed up with shady people, but she never asked, and he never said. It was just understood between the two of them that it wasn't to be discussed. And truthfully, his wife never much cared as long as the money kept flowing into the bank account.

Mark was a facilitator. He knew all the right people. And a lot of the wrong ones. Cirella's team was only a number of different ones that he used. It all depended on the job. Every crew he worked with had their own set of skills and talents. And some were more reliable than others. For the bigger jobs, Cirella's crew was at the top of the list. Mark usually operated in the shadows, not wanting to get caught up on any police radars. And he never went out on a job. He simply passed the info along for a piece of the action.

The two greeted each other and shook hands as Cirella got to the door. Mark invited him in, leading him into the family room so they could discuss business. They sat in a couple of chairs by the crackling fireplace across from each other.

"Suzy and the kids not here tonight?" Cirella asked.

"She took the girls out shopping."

"Uh oh. Three girls out shopping? Hope you're prepared for the bill."

The two men shared a laugh, with Mark throwing one hand up, resigned to whatever the cost was. "Eh, what are you gonna do? Suzy trained the girls well.

They're in high school now, always gotta have the latest fashions, you know?"

"Pretty soon they'll be trying to impress the boys, and you're gonna be sitting home at midnight on your front porch waiting for them."

Mark smiled. "I would never do that. I'd bring in you and your boys for that. Scare the bejeezus out of them."

Cirella grinned, thankful he didn't have those problems. "I'm glad I'll never have those issues."

"You never know, Dom, one of these days, some woman's gonna sweep you off your feet and then, wham, fast forward ten years and you got two kids."

"I kind of doubt it."

"We'll see about that. Anyway, let's get down to business."

"What? You didn't bring me here to have smores by the fire?" Cirella said with a laugh.

"Not hardly. Might have a job coming up for you in the next few days."

"What's the score?"

The amount they'd be taking was usually always the first question on Cirella's mind. Money first. Everything else, second. If the money wasn't good, nothing else would matter. If the money was there, then he'd start worrying about the possibilities, plans, and logistics of taking the haul. But usually if the money was good, Cirella would find a way to make it work. He wasn't against taking risks, but usually tried to avoid jobs if there was too great a chance of things going sideways. But the bigger the score, the more chances he was willing to take. Luckily, the job Mark was about to propose wasn't one of the riskier ones.

"I've been lining something up," Mark said. "Private residence. Security alarms. Probably some cameras. The whole property is completely fenced. Front gate only opens via a remote that Montgomery carries with him. Shouldn't be anything too tough for you and your boys to get through though."

"What's the score?"

"Greg Montgomery. Older guy, in his late sixties, very wealthy man. He's due to come back from a trip to Europe in a couple days. He'll be bringing back with him some jewelry and diamonds."

"How much?"

Mark contorted his face, not sure of a response. "Tough to say. Could be up to a million." Cirella raised an eyebrow, impressed with the take. He certainly was willing to listen to more. "At the very least, seven hundred and fifty. Depends on what he's got. I only know of the main ones, but he could have more."

"What's this guy do? Collector?"

"Investments mostly."

"Anything else on him?"

"He's most likely going to be stashing everything in a safe that he's got. Like I said, he's going to be coming back from Europe on a late-night flight, so he's not gonna have time to put it in the bank or a safety deposit box."

"So we got one shot at it."

"Yeah. I'll give you the address so you can stake the place out for a few days, figure out your plan. Then when I get the word he's on his way, I'll let you know."

"Sounds good," Cirella said. "What's the split?"

"I take twenty percent, you take the rest, split it with your guys however you want. I'll take care of my contacts giving me the information out of my share."

Cirella nodded. "Sounds like a deal."

"If there's anything else of value in the safe or anywhere else, grab it. If there's any cash lying around, it's yours, consider it a bonus."

Cirella smiled, liking it more by the minute. "Thanks."

"It's gonna take some time to get rid of everything, so you probably won't get your cut for a few weeks at least. Maybe a month."

"That's fine."

"But if you or any of your boys need an advance on the dough, let me know, and I can give you guys something and I'll just take it out on the back end."

"Should be able to wait."

Mark leaned forward in his chair and tapped Cirella on the knee. "Something else I wanna talk to you about."

Cirella also leaned forward, sensing the heaviness of the subject. "Yeah?"

"It's about Danny."

"What about him?"

"The last job you guys had a few weeks ago... it was a little hairier than it should've been. He beat a guy senseless when it wasn't necessary. The guy wasn't giving any problem from what everyone has said."

"I know it," Cirella replied. "He's been talked to."

"He brought unnecessary heat down on all of us, you more than anybody."

"I know. It won't happen again. He knows that."

"Good. 'Cause if there's one thing that you don't need... it's a loose cannon. He'll get you in deep. He'll get you so deep that one day you won't be able to get out."

"I'm on top of it."

"I hope so. You know I'm not someone who tries to stick his nose in where it don't belong. Your crew is your business. But when the jobs become harder than they should be, and things go sideways, then that affects my business. I'm only telling you this as a friend."

"And I appreciate that."

"You need to reel him in."

"I will."

"I hope so. 'Cause if you don't... someone's gonna reel you in."

2

———

Carter had come home about an hour later than usual. Stacy was already in the kitchen feeding the kids dinner. Upon hearing the door open, she looked over, seeing him walk in with a box of diapers under his arm.

"Sorry I'm late," Carter said. "Stopped at the store for diapers and some other things."

"It's OK. Kids were getting hungry so I figured I'd start feeding them."

Carter put the box of diapers down on the floor, then walked out of the house again. A minute later, he came back in with a few more bags, setting them down on the kitchen counter. He then left again to go back to his car. Curious, Stacy got up and went over to the counter to inspect the bags. There was formula, baby food, milk, and food. She then looked over at the door, hearing him come in again with several more bags tied to his hands. After he put them down on the counter as well, Stacy looked inside, seeing more food than she'd seen in a few weeks. As Carter brought in more bags and closed the door behind him, Stacy had more than a few questions for him.

"What's all this?"

"What's it look like?" Carter asked. "I went food shopping."

"With what money?"

"What're you, mad about having food?"

"No, I just want to know where the money came from. Two days ago we talked about this and we had fifty dollars in our account. I know all this cost a lot more than fifty dollars, and I don't see a receipt in any of these bags."

"What? You think I stole it or something?"

Stacy shrugged. "You tell me."

"One of the guys at work loaned me a hundred dollars."

Stacy wasn't sure that was the truth but decided to play along. "When do you have to pay it back?"

"Whenever. He said if I give a little back each week that was fine. So even if I just give him twenty bucks a week for the next five weeks that should be OK."

As Stacy started unpacking everything and putting the food in the cabinets and refrigerator, Carter sat at the table and continued feeding and interacting with the kids. After Stacy was done, she turned around and just looked at her husband talking to their kids. He was a good father, she thought. She knew he would do anything for their family. He was hands-on with the kids, played with them, changed diapers, got up in the middle of the night, there wasn't one complaint she had about him. If not for their money problems, everything would be just about perfect.

After a few moments, Stacy sat at the table also. "I heard back today from those two jobs I applied for."

"And?"

A frown came over her face and she shook her head. "I didn't get it."

"Without even getting an interview?"

"I think one of them already had a few part-time workers, and they just promoted one of them," Stacy said. "And the other one already hired somebody."

"Something else will come along."

"It's just frustrating."

"I know. But we'll be OK." Carter leaned across the table and kissed his wife. "We'll be OK."

CIRELLA HAD GOTTEN word from Mark several hours earlier that Montgomery would be coming home that night. He immediately called his crew and they all met at the diner, like they usually did before a job, so they could all go over the plan.

"How much time we got?" Brantly asked.

"Probably about six hours," Cirella answered. "Plane should be touching down about five hours from now, then roughly an hour for him to get home."

"Do we know if he's travelling with anyone?" Rollins asked.

"Last word I got was that he was alone. Now who knows if that will change or not, but it shouldn't affect us too much. Even if he's got somebody, it shouldn't be more than one, maybe two other people at the most."

"Almost seems too easy," Falk said.

"Listen," Cirella said, tapping Falk on the arm since he was sitting next to him. "We got enough guys to get the job done and get the drop on them. There should be no need to beat anyone senseless or kill anyone, right? Get in, do the job, and get out. That's it. Nothing more."

"There is that guard on the front gate."

"What, are you kidding me? Rent-a-cop. Probably never even fired a gun in his life. He's easy. Should be no problem."

"What about the old man?" Falk asked, almost hoping to find a problem somewhere so he could go ballistic on someone.

"Guy's pushing seventy," Cirella said, motioning with a coffee in his hand. "How much trouble could he be? He's a businessman, what's he gonna do, go all Chuck Norris on us?"

"Never know."

"Everything will be fine as long as everyone keeps their heads on straight and doesn't panic. This should be a nice, easy job. We're professionals. There should be no mistakes."

After finishing up their meals, the men got in their cars and drove to their storage unit. It was there that they stored their weapons, guns, ammunition, as well as a black SUV that they used on jobs. They didn't think it was a good idea to be using their personal vehicles on jobs, as eventually someone would spot it, leading the authorities right to them. But with this, when the job was over, they parked it back in the storage unit, out of sight. Unless they were followed there, no one would ever know it was there or connect it to them.

Once inside the unit, they closed the door and put the light on, changing into dark colored clothes. They each had their own black duffel bag that they took with them, carrying guns, ammunition, masks, and anything else they thought they might need. Isaac was the wheel man and usually drove. He was hands-down the best driver of the bunch. He could weave in and out of traffic, get out of jams – which he'd done several times – better than anybody. Cirella was usually in the front passenger seat that way he could see what was happening. Rollins and Falk were the sharpshooters, probably the best shots of the bunch, though Rollins also was the best at getting into tight spots. He was good with explosives and getting through locked doors.

Once they were all ready, they drove to the Montgomery home. They'd staked the place out for the last couple of nights, so they were familiar with the grounds and already had a plan in place for how to enter. It was a big property, several acres at least, with a tall black fence that went around it, a guard and gate stationed at the front. The crew parked their SUV a little further down the road, just sitting there until they saw Montgomery's car drive past them. Mark had given them a picture of the vehicle they were looking for, so they were aware of what it looked like. Only a few minutes after they arrived, Cirella got a phone call.

"Hey, plane just touched down," Mark said. "Your bird's on the way."

"Got it." Cirella put his phone back in his pocket and let the others know. "Target's on the way."

Everyone reached into their bag and removed their guns. Each had an assault rifle, and all of them carried a backup pistol just in case.

"Noah, you're up," Cirella said.

"Wait, I thought that was my job," Falk replied.

"I changed it. Noah."

"Right," Rollins said, exiting the SUV.

"What's going on?" Falk asked.

"Nothing," Cirella answered. "I just think Noah's the best to handle that."

Falk was a little peeved, thinking he got passed over. "Why?"

"Because I'm in charge, that's why."

"Dominic..."

"Listen, you have a lot of muscle and you like to use it. This is a job that requires some finesse. I really would prefer getting out of here without having to worry about a body count."

Falk didn't reply, but he was steaming. He just looked out his window and shook his head. He moved his mouth and jaw around, clearly unhappy with the developments. The plan was that a few minutes after Montgomery arrived, they would drive up to the gate, and as soon as the guard came out to check them out, Rollins would come up behind him and subdue him. There were a bunch of trees and shrubs that lined the front of the property that were thick enough to easily conceal somebody's movements.

Cirella worried that Falk would use too much force that wasn't necessary. Outside of Falk, the other three were much more cautious. They were afraid or hesitant to beat someone down, or kill them if necessary, but only if it threatened their ability to escape. Robberies were one thing. Murder was another. Killing people brought more heat. More heat than they wanted. They would do it if they had to, but only as a last resort.

Sometimes, they felt that Falk went looking for trouble instead of just playing things nice and easy. He'd shot five people over the last two years, killed three of them, and physically assaulted several others, putting a few of them in the hospital. He'd also raped two women over the past year, though that was unknown to the rest of the team. Falk was a big guy, standing over six foot three, and solidly built, and he liked to use his muscle as much as possible.

With Rollins waiting in the bushes, easily concealed by all the foliage, the rest of the team was sitting patiently in the truck, anticipating their target coming soon. Falk, though, was letting his mind wander elsewhere as he stewed in the back seat. He always thought Cirella was harder on him than the rest of the boys, and it was beginning to irritate him, believing that he got picked on unnecessarily. He felt like Cirella yelled at him more just because he wasn't one of the original members of the team, and he never really developed a full amount of trust in him. Falk was starting to think he'd be better off on his own, not having to worry about anyone giving him orders. Though the money had been pretty good as a member on Cirella's crew, Falk was more worried about being treated well. And he didn't think Cirella would ever do that.

About half an hour later, they crouched down in their seats, seeing the bright lights of Montgomery's car lighting up the road.

"All right, this is it," Cirella said. "Everyone get ready."

The men all checked their weapons and were ready to go.

"How soon?" Brantly asked.

"Give him a few minutes to get settled."

"Wouldn't it make sense to hit him as soon as he gets in the door? We can get him before he has a chance to put the stuff in the safe. Then we don't have to worry about it."

"Yeah, but if we hit too soon and he sees us coming, he's got a chance to hit the alarm and then we stirred up a hornet's nest. Let's just give him some time to relax and get comfortable."

"He won't have a chance to hit the alarm if we take him out right away," Falk said. "Let's get it over with."

"We'll wait a few minutes," Cirella said.

They waited about twenty minutes, giving Montgomery plenty of time to put his diamonds and jewelry into his safe.

"All right, let's hit it," Cirella said, nudging Brantly on the arm.

"You got it."

"Nice and slow. No panic."

Brantly slowly drove down the street, turning into the driveway that led up to the Montgomery estate, stopping just in front of the gate. An armed guard came out of the guard house to approach the SUV.

"Everybody steady," Cirella quietly said.

"Help you guys?" the guard asked, just as he got to the driver's side window. The man had no sooner asked the question when Rollins had slipped out of the bushes and snuck up behind him. He already had his mask on so none of the security cameras would pick up his face. Rollins grabbed hold of the man's arms, making sure the guard couldn't get to his gun. Falk quickly exited the car, also having his mask on, and rushed over to the two men struggling, giving his teammate a hand. Falk immediately drove the butt end of his rifle into the man's midsection, the guard hunching over and instantly struggling for air as he lost his breath. Falk let loose with a few right hands to the man's face, causing the guard to fall over. They then dragged the man back into the guard house, tying him up once he was inside.

"Turn the lights off," Cirella said, Brantly complying with the directive. "He doesn't need to see us coming." The two of them also put their masks on, not wanting to do it yet and alarm the guard when he approached the car.

Once Rollins and Falk had tied the guard up good and tight, making sure there was no chance the man could get loose, Rollins opened up the gate, letting the others drive through. Rollins and Falk then followed the SUV on foot, closing the gate behind them as the car slowly drove up to the house. The two men then ran up to the house, meeting Cirella and Brantly as they got out of the car.

"You guys know what to do," Cirella said.

Already having the layout of the house, they split up into two pairs. Cirella and Brantly would go through the front while Rollins and Falk would enter the house through a side window. Each team broke a window to make an entrance into the house, and once inside, knew they didn't have a lot of time. They knew a silent alarm was already going off. Since Montgomery lived alone, at least they didn't have to worry about encountering anybody else. The house was dark, but they could hear Montgomery moving around upstairs, opening and closing doors, flicking lights on and off. They rushed up to steps, going down the hallway until they reached Montgomery's office, and considering the light was still on, figured the man was still inside.

All four men stood just outside the door, which was halfway open, looking to Cirella for the sign to move. Cirella motioned to Brantly to stay put and stand guard outside the door, just in case they had unexpected visitors. Cirella put three fingers up for the rest of the guys, indicating they were going into the room in three seconds. He then pulled a finger down, then another one, then pointed at the room. They were ready to go.

Cirella forced the door open as he led the charge into the room. Montgomery was sitting at his desk, writing something, when he nearly jumped out of his chair, startled at seeing men, clad in all black clothing, including masks, coming through the door. Cirella kept his gun pointed at Montgomery as Rollins and Falk looked around the room to make sure nobody else was there.

"Who are you?" Montgomery asked. "What do you want? How'd you get into my house?"

"Listen, you got two choices," Cirella said, sounding tough. "You can live or you can die. If you wanna live, give us the diamonds and jewelry you just brought back. If you wanna die, we'll still take them anyway, so you might as well take the easier option."

Montgomery still looked a little stunned. Now all three guns were pointed at him. Cirella knew they didn't have all day to wait for him to make a decision since there was a good chance the police had already been called from the alarm going off.

"If you don't make the right decision in ten seconds, we're just gonna blow a hole through you and look for it ourselves," Cirella said. "And we have an expert safecracker, so don't think you can hold out."

Cirella started counting down, starting at ten. He got down to two before Montgomery finally gave in.

"OK. How do I know you won't kill me anyway?"

"There's no reason to," Cirella answered. "You don't know us, can't identify us, can't hurt us. Just be cool, don't do anything stupid, and you'll live to see another day."

Montgomery sighed, hating to see himself lose what he just spent the last few weeks in Europe trying to acquire. But it was better to lose his diamonds than to lose his life.

"Fine," Montgomery said. "You win."

"Where are they?" Cirella asked.

"In my safe."

"Get them."

Montgomery got up from his chair and turned around, removing a picture on the wall that was directly behind him, revealing a medium-sized safe. He took another look at the men behind him, still with guns on him, and shook his head. He thought having a bunch of armed guards with him would have drawn unwanted attention to himself. He should have done things differently, he thought. At the very least, he thought he should have waited another day, coming back in the daytime, where he could have immediately put his jewels in a safety deposit box. He was doing a lot of second guessing as he turned the dials on his safe, not that any of it mattered much at the moment. There was nothing he could do about it now except live with it.

Once the last number clicked, Montgomery pulled the safe open. He took a look back at the masked men, then put his hand inside the safe. Thinking he was reaching for a gun, Falk opened up, firing several shots into Montgomery's back. The elderly man immediately slumped to the floor, eventually landing face down at his final resting spot.

Cirella angrily pulled off his mask, immediately looking at Falk. "What the hell are you doing?"

"He was reaching for a gun!" Falk replied, also pulling his mask off, pointing toward the safe.

Rollins quickly rushed to the safe and looked

inside. He then looked back at Cirella and shook his head. There was no gun to be found. That was enough to send Cirella over the edge. He charged at Falk, wrestling him down to the floor, Cirella on top of him, clenching the collar of Falk's shirt and shaking him. Rollins had started emptying the safe's contents into his bag, but looked back when he heard the commotion. He let the bag drop to the ground as he hurried over to the men, worried that Cirella was going to do something he might regret.

"Isaac!" Rollins yelled, knowing he'd need help in separating the two men.

Brantly charged into the room, pulling Cirella off their teammate. Falk quickly got up, ready for the fight to continue, but Rollins stepped in front of him, making sure it stopped right then and there.

"We don't have time for this," Rollins said, looking at both combatants.

"He's right," Brantly said. "We gotta go."

Cirella looked at the men and nodded, quickly getting himself composed again. It was a rare slip-up for him, who prided himself at staying under control at all times, under any circumstance. It was the amateurs who lost control. That was one of the reasons he believed they were so successful. They were unflappable and just rolled with whatever came along. They didn't cave to pressure or when something went wrong.

"All right," Cirella said. "Finish unloading the safe and let's go."

Rollins and Brantly went over to the safe and cleaned it out. While they were doing that, Cirella and Falk were busy giving each other evil glances. If they weren't under the gun to leave, there was a good chance one of them wouldn't be walking out of there.

"We're good!" Rollins shouted, putting the last of the jewelry into his bag.

"Let's go," Cirella replied.

The men all put their masks back on to avoid getting their faces caught on a camera somewhere. They raced down the stairs and out of the house, quickly jumping back into their car. They drove back down to the gate where Rollins once again got out to open it. Once he was back inside, Brantly floored it, making sure they got out of the area as quickly as possible. Cirella removed his mask and put his window down just a crack to listen for sirens. The police were on the way and would probably get there in less than a minute judging from how close they sounded.

Once they'd safely turned down a few streets and were sure they were in the clear, Cirella's thoughts returned to the mess they'd just left. He started shaking his head and mumbling, saying every curse word he knew, and even making a few up. He couldn't believe such an easy job turned into this. The heat was going to be on them even more now, maybe even making Mark's job more difficult in getting rid of the stuff they stole. It was one thing to be involved in a robbery, but now it was a murder rap. Everybody would be out in full force on this. Cirella wiped his face, not being able to think of anything except the body they just left behind. He couldn't just let this be. Falk was becoming too much of a wild card that he just couldn't deal with or trust him anymore. Something was going to have to change.

3

Once the crew finally got back to the storage unit, they parked the car, closed the door, and got out of the vehicle. Cirella was still steaming. He slammed the door shut, walked completely around to the other side of the car, ready to confront Falk. Falk had just gotten out and saw Cirella approaching, though he didn't figure he was coming to continue their confrontation from earlier. Falk had a cocky-looking grin on his face, like he was proud of everything that happened that night. Cirella walked straight up to him and unleashed a thunderous right hand, knocking Falk off his feet.

"What the hell were you doing?" Cirella asked. "You stupid son of a bitch!"

Brantly and Rollins quickly went over to the pair to try to prevent a full-blown fight from happening. Rollins came up behind Cirella and grabbed his arms.

Falk quickly got back to his feet to continue the fracas but Brantly rushed in, standing in front of him to keep him from getting at their leader.

"What's your problem?" Falk asked.

"What's my problem?" Cirella replied. "What's my problem?! You're my problem. You're a damned idiot. You really thought a sixty-nine-year-old man was a threat to us? You stupid punk."

"I thought he was reaching for a gun! What was I supposed to do?!"

"Wait until you have visual confirmation that he was a threat. That's what you're supposed to do. Try acting like a professional for once instead of some two-bit punk kid who's doing his first job."

"All that matters is that we did the job, we got what we were supposed to, and we're getting paid. That's it. That's all that matters. All the rest is just noise."

Cirella tried to wrestle himself free from Rollins' clutches so he could get a few more shots in on Falk, but he wasn't able to.

"Get out of my sight," Cirella said.

"What?" Falk asked.

"Just get out of my sight. Get out. I don't wanna see your face."

To try to diffuse things further, Brantly gently gave Falk a push to get him moving. "C'mon, man, let's just give him some time to calm down."

"What? You siding with him?" Falk said.

"I'm not siding with anybody. I'm just trying to get

everyone to relax. It's still fresh, let's just give it a day or two for everyone to unwind."

Falk didn't even bother getting changed back into his regular clothes. The group came in two separate cars from the diner, Cirella and Rollins, and Brantly and Falk.

"Just go to the car, and I'll take you home," Brantly said.

Falk walked out and headed to the car, pretty angry himself at once again being questioned by their supposed leader. Just par for the course, he thought.

"I'll take him home," Brantly said. "What do you want me to do after that?"

"Just go home and take it easy," Cirella calmly said. "I gotta talk things over with Mark, then I'll call you."

"Sounds good."

After the other two left, Cirella and Rollins changed back into their normal clothes, then started discussing the night's events.

"Tell me something," Cirella said. "Did you think Montgomery was pulling a gun?"

Rollins thought for a second, deciding whether he wanted to try to cover up for his teammate and place peacemaker, or tell the truth, even though Cirella wouldn't like it, and might serve as a catalyst to shake things up. In the end, he decided to just come clean. It was a rule amongst the group to not lie to each other over anything. No matter what it was, good news, bad news, or indifferent, they had to be honest with each other.

"No. You were on the side where the door opened up, so you couldn't see, but I had a straight line of sight. I could see there was no gun."

"What was he reaching for?"

"He was gonna grab the bag of diamonds and pull it out."

Cirella looked down at the ground and shook his head. Anger was coming back to him again. "Did he have the same view?"

"Well, he was on the other side of me, probably with the best view of all of us. I don't think there's any doubt about it. He knew what was going on. He could see it."

"He just didn't care," Cirella said.

"I think he just felt like shooting the guy."

"This can't go on. It can't keep happening. He's gonna put us all back in the joint."

"I dunno, Dom, part of me feels like... if we go down for stuff that we do, fine, that's on us. But I don't wanna go down for shit that he's doing. Why should all of us take murder raps just because he's got some kind of macho complex going on?"

Cirella nodded. "You're right."

"It seems like he's getting worse as time goes on. He wasn't like this in the beginning. Now? Seems like he's looking for something or someone to get into it with. It's almost like he's feeding off it, trying to see how many bodies he can leave behind. I mean, say what you want about us, that's never been our style. We do what we have to and no more. Killing people just for the sake of killing isn't our bag. And I'm not sure I want any part of it anymore."

Cirella continued to nod, soaking everything in. Everything Rollins was saying lined up with his own thoughts. It was just nice to hear the same point of view from someone else sometimes. And he couldn't let Falk drive a wedge through the team. They were a close-knit group before Falk came, they still would be after he was gone. Cirella couldn't let Rollins or Brantly bail on the squad if they had enough of Falk too, and judging from the conversation with Rollins, they had.

"I'm gonna go talk to Mark," Cirella said.

"What? Tonight? Why don't you get some rest first?"

Cirella shrugged. "It's not like we just ran a marathon. Might as well talk it over with him and let him know what happened while it's fresh in my mind. Besides, there's a dead body. He's gonna need to know."

They left the storage facility, with Cirella dropping Rollins off at his apartment before driving to Mark's home. Cirella had already sent Mark a message to let him know he was coming. Cirella visiting Mark directly after a job wasn't really all that unusual. He'd done it often unless there was a specific reason not to. The one thing Cirella didn't do was let Mark know how it went. Usually if a job went off without a hitch, Cirella indicated as such. When he didn't say anything that was usually a clue to Mark that something went wrong.

Mark was waiting by the front door again when Cirella finally arrived. Since his wife and kids were inside, Mark had his friend follow him around the side of the house until they got to the large deck in the back. Before beginning their conversation, Mark lit a fire in the brick outdoor fireplace as Cirella sat down. Once Mark joined him, they began discussing business.

"How'd everything go?"

Cirella squeezed his nose, then wiped his mouth, not really wanting to say. "Well, there were some complications."

"Did he have all the stuff?"

"Oh yeah. It's all here."

Cirella had the black bag with him that they put everything from Montgomery's safe into. He unzipped the bag and slid it over to Mark so he could take a look at it. Mark took a few minutes to inspect the merchandise, impressed with the quality of the diamonds and jewelry. It was just as beautiful as was described to him.

"So if everything's here, what's the problem?" Mark asked.

"Problem is Montgomery's dead."

Mark immediately took his eyes off the merchandise and stared at Cirella. He then calmly put the stuff back in the bag, though his face gave off a look of obvious displeasure.

"What happened? He put up a struggle?"

Cirella looked away at some nearby trees, shook his head, and threw his hands up. "Shouldn't have happened. Shouldn't have happened."

"What went down?"

"Got into the house, no problem. Everything went off without a hitch. Surprised Montgomery in his office and he agreed to open the safe. He opened it, reached inside, and Falk mowed him down."

"Was he reaching for a gun?"

"Falk said he was," Cirella answered. "Rollins said they both had clear angles of the safe and there was no gun in sight... and there was no gun in the safe, we checked."

"This complicates things."

"I know."

"Gonna be more heat on everyone now. Getting rid of the stuff is going to be a little more difficult."

"I'm just so pissed off," Cirella said. "It didn't need to happen. Didn't need to happen."

"What'd I tell you about him? I told you he'd be your downfall."

"I could've killed him. I still might."

"I don't think I have to tell you that this creates a lot of issues. And I don't just mean with this job. Eventually the heat will die down and I'll be able to get rid of the stuff, but the long-term implications for you and your crew, that's another matter entirely."

Cirella knew what he was implying. He didn't need it spelled out for him. He and his crew would soon be considered a liability, a risk, because they had a loose cannon on board.

"How am I supposed to keep throwing jobs your way if I can't be sure how it's gonna turn out?" Mark asked.

Cirella nodded. "I understand."

"Like I told you before, your crew is your business, and I won't tell you how to handle your own business, but I think you know what has to be done."

"I'll get it taken care of. He's not gonna bring us down."

"I would hope not. It would be rather unfortunate if he did."

"If I have to go with a three-man team, then we will."

"What about just adding another guy in his place?"

Cirella seemed lukewarm to the idea. "Hard to have another guy just step in. Depends on the job, I guess. Gotta develop trust, know what and how he thinks, what he'll do in certain situations. Last thing I wanna do is rush into it and bring in another new guy and have him turn out to be just like the guy we're replacing."

"Trust is a big issue."

"Major issue," Cirella said.

The two of them sat there silently for a few minutes, enjoying the fire and nighttime air.

"What about that other kid?" Mark blurted out.

"What kid?"

"Your original guy. Carter. What about bringing him back in the fold?"

Cirella made a face like it wouldn't be so easy, indicating it was unlikely. "I dunno, I kind of think not."

"Why not? What's he doing these days? Talk to him lately?"

"Haven't talked to him in a while. Few years at least. Not since we all got sent up."

"He was a reliable guy if I can recall."

"Very reliable," Cirella said. "Would love to have him back if he was interested."

"Why not give him a call?"

"He started up a family. That was one of the reasons he wanted to give it up. Wanted to settle down with his girl."

"Well, we all know how families go sometimes, right?"

"How's that?"

"Sometimes they have a habit of separating," Mark replied. "Might be worth your while to check it out."

"Yeah. Maybe I will."

"In any case, in regards to Danny, how do you think he'll handle it?"

"Same way he handles everything. Not well."

4

C irella had spent most of the day checking into Carter's backstory. Cirella knew some guys who were good with computers and employed one of them to dig up as much information as they could on Carter from the last few years. Cirella got a report on everything that his former teammate and friend had been doing: his job, his family, his mortgage, his financial situation, it was almost like running a credit report. It was pretty obvious to Cirella that Carter had been struggling the last year or two, which could only help Cirella when he came calling.

But for now, Cirella had something more pressing on his mind. He'd already told the others that he was cutting Falk loose, now he just had to tell the man himself. Cirella didn't always carry a gun with him, just in case he was stopped by the police on some trumped-up charge, but he made sure he carried one with him now. Just in case. There was no telling how Falk would take the news, but Cirella made sure he was well prepared.

Cirella waited until it was dark, having spent the previous few hours talking to Brantly and Rollins, as well as checking on Carter's story. It was well after ten by the time Cirella got to Falk's apartment. It was a medium-sized apartment complex, with several hundred units there. There were about twenty buildings in all, with each building housing about twenty units, each building separated by either grass or parking spaces. There were only two floors, one tenant lived on the bottom, another lived on top, and each had their own walk-out door. Falk lived on a first-floor end unit. Cirella didn't bother to tell Falk he was coming, not wanting him to fly off the handle if he suspected bad news was coming. Cirella thought it'd be better to just surprise him with the news.

As Cirella walked up the concrete pathway to the apartment which was lit up by solar powered lights, he could hear voices coming from Falk's apartment. One of which he could tell was Falk's, the other sounded like a woman. Cirella didn't care if he was alone or not though. He continued his trek to the door and put his ear up to it, just listening to what was going on inside. There was a lot of laughing and grunting and fooling around.

After a minute, Cirella curled up his fist and pounded on the door. There was anger in his knock.

He noticed the curtains moving, most likely Falk checking to see who it was. A few seconds later, the door opened up, Falk standing there in just his boxers.

"Dom. What's up?" Falk said, flashing a smile.

Falk had a beer in his hand and his eyes were glossy. It was quite obvious he'd had a few too many. Cirella could tell by the way he was standing, swaying from side to side ever so slightly. He wasn't sure if Falk's being inebriated would wind up helping or hurting, but in the end it didn't really matter. He was ready for anything.

"Mind if I come in?" Cirella asked.

"Sure. Sure." Falk stumbled back a step or two and put his free arm out. "Come on in. Mi casa es su casa."

"Thanks." Cirella stepped inside the apartment. He noticed an open bag of what he assumed was cocaine on the table by the couch.

Falk closed the door behind him. "Hey, baby, get my buddy a drink."

Cirella put his arms up. "No, no, I'm good. Thanks."

"So, what's up? We got another job coming up?"

Cirella glanced at the scantily clad woman who was only wearing a bra and a thong. "Tell the girl to take a hike."

"What? Why? She brightens up the room."

"'Cause we don't discuss business in front of other people."

"Oh, OK, OK. Hey, babe, why don't you go into the bedroom and take those things off?" Falk said, a lusty look in his eye. "I'll be in in a few minutes to help you with it."

The woman did as she was told and walked into the bedroom, both men looking at her as she disappeared.

Falk tapped Cirella on the arm. "Not bad, huh?"

"Yeah, nice."

"Picked her up at a bar a couple hours ago. She's a real knockout."

"Yeah, real pretty."

"So, what's up?" Falk asked, plopping himself down on an oversized plush chair.

"You know I'm not real big on long-winded speeches or anything, so I'm just gonna make this short and sweet. I've been talking to a lot of people over the past twenty-four hours, Mark, the other boys, and we've come to the conclusion that you're too much of a wild card."

Falk took a drink, then squinted his eyes, trying to decipher what he was being told. He leaned forward in his seat to look at Cirella a little more clearly. "What are you saying?"

"I'm saying you're done. You're through. You're not part of the team anymore."

Anger started flowing through Falk's veins. He stood up and tossed the beer bottle on the floor. "What do you mean I'm through? Nobody fires me. Nobody."

"Fine. Then consider it as us going our separate ways. An amicable divorce."

"What's this about? Just because I killed that old man?"

"It's about a lot of things. That old man was just the tip of the iceberg. It's about the killings, the beatings, going off course, not sticking to the plan, doing your own things, all of that. And it's been going on for over a year now. It's obvious you don't want to be part of the team anymore."

Even though Falk had already been thinking about going off on his own anyway, it was the suddenness of being told he was being kicked out that was making him mad. He wanted to be the one to say when he was done, nobody else.

"I'll leave the team when I'm good and ready," Falk said.

"You got no say in it. You're done."

"Nobody tells me I'm done."

"I just did."

Falk dropped his arms and was ready to start throwing hands.. He then reached back and took a healthy swing with his right hand at Cirella's face who easily sidestepped the blow. Now Cirella was the one angry. He was always thought to be level-headed, calm, especially in the face of adversity, but he really didn't have much of a leash at the moment, especially in Falk's case.

After getting out of the way of Falk's attempted punch, Cirella nailed him with a left jab. Temporarily stunned, Cirella didn't waste any time in continuing the assault. He kept hitting Falk, mostly with a forceful and powerful right hand. It turned out to be a little easier than Cirella would have expected. Maybe it was because Falk wasn't in his normal state with however much he'd been drinking, but he really didn't put up much of a fight. Cirella didn't care though. He didn't care at all that it really wasn't a fair fight in his opponent's condition. Right now was all about unleashing all of the anger that he had been storing up inside about his former teammate.

Even in his drunken and now badly beaten state, Falk kept getting up after being knocked down. After several minutes of the beating, Cirella was getting tired of it, not to mention his hand was beginning to hurt from repeatedly smashing it into Falk's face. Wanting to end the fight once and for all, Cirella picked up the beer bottle with the intention of smashing it over Falk's face, hoping that would render him unconscious. As soon as he picked it up, the woman came running out of the bedroom after hearing all the commotion. She saw Falk lying on the floor at first, though he'd now gotten to his knees, and she screamed.

"What are you doing?!" she yelled at Cirella.

"Get back in there!" Cirella shouted, pointing at the bedroom.

Cirella, seeing that Falk was getting back to his feet, turned his back to the woman, which for some strange reason, made her feel brave enough that she could do something to stop him from hitting the man she came home with. She ran over to Cirella and jumped on his back, not really sure what to do after that, probably hoping that she distracted him long enough for Falk to get back to his feet and help her out. It didn't work, though, as Cirella grabbed a clump of her brown hair and pulled her over his shoulder, causing her to scream in pain. As she fell hard on the floor on her backside, Falk had finally gotten to his feet. Cirella delivered another punch, sending Falk to one knee again. Cirella then looked around for the bottle and picked it up. With a firm grip, Cirella raised the bottle over his head, then quickly brought it back down in one swift motion, striking Falk on the top of his head. The bottle shattered into large pieces, opening up a pretty good-sized cut on Falk's head. It did the trick, though, as Falk finally slumped to the ground for good.

Cirella checked Falk's pulse, and though he was still breathing, he was no longer an issue. At least not on this night. Falk knew where the whole team lived, and it wouldn't have surprised Cirella if he tried to get even one night. He hoped not. He hoped that this would be a wake-up call to Falk, and that he would get the message. Something told Cirella that he wouldn't, but at least he tried. He could have just killed Falk and been done with it, but he wanted to at least give him the opportunity to walk away without incident.

Cirella left the apartment, satisfied with the conclusion. Though he hoped it wouldn't have come to blows, it was what it was. And now it was done with.

He called Brantly and Rollins to let them know what happened. Though both of them knew the exile of Falk had to be done for the betterment of the team, they each expressed concern about the state of the group now. They could function as a three-man team for some jobs, but having that fourth man really made things easier. Heck, they wouldn't have been opposed to adding a fifth man to the team for some extra support. But having four really would have been ideal.

"You got any other ideas besides Jack?" Rollins asked.

"Eh, I put a few feelers out, but I really want to talk to Jack first," Cirella said. "If we can get him on board again, nothing else matters."

"Might be a tough sell. He's been out for a while. Especially if he's still with Stacy, she's not gonna want him to come back."

"Yeah, well, money problems have a way of making people do things that they really don't want to or thought they wouldn't."

"And you're sure they're struggling?"

"Reports I got indicate they've been late paying multiple bills. Now, as far as I know, people who are OK financially usually pay everything on time."

"So when you gonna ask him?"

"Well, I wanna be subtle about it," Cirella said. "Work my way back in slowly. We don't have any other jobs lined up right now, so we don't need to rush it. I don't wanna just show up at his door and ask him to join the crew again. Might get a door slammed in my face." Cirella laughed.

"What if Mark comes up with a job soon?"

"After what happened on the job we just had, I'm pretty sure we're not gonna be first on his speed dial."

5

Since Jack was working, and it was a nice, pleasant day outside, Stacy took the kids to the park for a bit. She had hoped that walking around for a while would help to clear her mind and ease some of her tension. By the time she got home and pulled into the driveway, she noticed some boxes by the front door. The kids had fallen asleep in the car on the way home, so Stacy went up to the door to see what was there. There were five big boxes of diapers and a case of formula.

A brief smile came over Stacy's face, happy and relieved to see even the most basic of supplies, but her mind immediately thought to where it had come from. She figured it was unlikely to be from Jack since he was working and usually didn't come home when he was on break. She also always checked their bank account every day out of the unrealistic hope that an unexpected deposit would come through even though she knew their situation wasn't changing. And their credit cards were maxed out. So she knew that it wasn't something that was ordered online.

After carrying the kids inside and laying them down, Stacy started trying to get down to the bottom of the mystery. There were no shipping labels on the boxes, so she knew they weren't ordered online. Someone dropped them off. The first call she made was to her parents, thinking they may have been in the area and wanted to surprise them or something. Stacy had previously indicated to them that they were struggling a little, though she hadn't yet let on just how much.

Stacy spoke to her mother for about ten minutes, and after her mom told her that they didn't leave anything for them, Stacy then texted Jack a message to let him know about the packages. It took about twenty minutes for Jack to respond, but he claimed to have no idea either. Knowing Jack's background before they got together, Stacy didn't like the thoughts entering her mind. She wondered if her husband was starting to revert back to former tendencies out of desperation and trying to keep it a secret from her.

When Jack got come a few hours later, he was greeted with a kiss from his wife, and then he hugged his children. Stacy showed him the boxes that were at the door, and judging by the look on his face, he was as surprised as she was. He honestly had no idea where

they came from. He insisted it wasn't him. She believed
him.

"Who would have done this?" Stacy asked.

Jack just shook his head, not having a good answer.
"I really don't know."

"I guess we should just be thankful for it."

Jack didn't reply, but he was probably more skeptical than most people. Maybe because of his background, but he didn't believe most people did things
out of the kindness of their hearts. There was always
an angle to be played. Something to be had in return
for their generosity. He wasn't sure this would be any
different.

After they ate dinner, Jack played with the kids in
the living room as Stacy went on their computer to
look at bills. Jack heard her mumbling for a few
minutes but didn't pay much attention to it, as he
figured it was just her being frustrated at the amounts
she was looking at. It was a usual occurrence at their
house. But this time was different.

"Jack…," Stacy said, the uncertainty in her voice
clearly evident.

Jack made sure the kids were busy playing with
blocks before he came over to the desk. "What?" he
asked, not really wanting to hear how badly they were
struggling.

"Umm, I don't understand what's going on here."

"What do you mean?"

"I mean our bills are paid."

"What?" Jack asked, assuming there must have been a mistake.

"Our bills are already paid for the month."

"That can't be."

"That's what I thought, but look," Stacy said, pointing at the monitor.

Jack looked at the screen and saw the confirmation for himself. Stacy pulled up bill after bill, changing the websites... water bill, electric, phones, car payment, even their mortgage. Everything was caught up and up to date.

"What's going on?" Stacy asked.

"I..." Jack was having a hard time explaining it himself. How could he explain something that he didn't know about? He had no idea what was going on either.

"Did you get a lot of money recently that you didn't tell me about?"

Jack put his arms up to express his innocence. "I swear, I have no idea what's going on. I didn't pay these."

"Then who did?"

Jack shrugged, still not having a good response. "I don't know."

"Why would someone just pay our bills for us?"

"I don't know."

"I wonder if it's the same person who dropped off the diapers and formula?"

"Might be."

"Could it be someone from your work?" Stacy asked.

"No, I haven't told anyone we were behind on bills or anything."

"What about the person you borrowed the money from?"

Jack rubbed the back of his neck, hesitating to answer. Stacy could tell by his face that he was hiding something.

"Jack..."

"It's nothing."

"What is it?" Stacy asked, though she had a good idea what he was holding back. "You didn't actually borrow the money from someone, did you?"

Jack sighed. "No."

"Jack...," Stacy said, clearly exasperated. "What did you do?"

"I did what I had to do."

"Did you steal that stuff?"

"No, I did not."

"Then what?"

"I paid someone else for most of it."

Stacy wasn't sure she understood. "What do you mean you paid someone else?"

"Well, there's a guy I know who has stuff that he sells. For a discount."

"So it is stolen."

Jack shrugged again. "I don't know, maybe. I don't know where he gets it from."

"Nobody sells that stuff for a discount unless they got it for free."

Jack knew that was the case but didn't want to admit it. If you don't ask, and you don't know for sure, then you can pretend that it's all legit.

"Listen, I don't want to resort to those kinds of things," he said. "But I will if I have to. If that's our only option, then I'll take it."

Stacy stood up and gave her husband a hug and a kiss. "I don't want you doing stuff like that again. Promise?"

Jack just looked at her and smiled, nodding, though the words never left his lips.

"When you left that life behind, we said we'd get through this together, for better or worse. And we will."

"That was before we had two kids who depend on us," Jack said.

"You think we'll ever find out who did all this?"

"I don't know. I get the feeling we eventually will."

CIRELLA HAD JUST ARRIVED at Mark's home, just as he was asked to. Mark almost always did business out of his home, not wanting to take the chance of being spotted in a public place with the people he did business with, since most of them had a record. At least at his home, Mark knew the discussions would remain private. There was always a chance that one of his contacts would be followed there, though Mark gave them instructions that if they had even the slightest inkling that they were being tailed, to break it off. But even in the odd chance that the police did trail someone to his house, it didn't prove anything. But still, Mark wanted to stay out of the police and federal eye if at all possible.

Once inside, Cirella and Mark went into the study to talk. The room was adorned with paintings on the wall, bookshelves loaded with books, a fireplace, and several comfy chairs. Mark turned the fireplace on as he usually did. Though the gas fireplace didn't have quite the same feel as the crackling sound of the wood ones, he still loved the ambience of it.

"Didn't think we'd be meeting again so soon," Cirella said.

"You know how things go in this business. Sometimes things move fast and in unexpected directions."

"Yeah."

"How'd things go with Danny? You talk to him yet?"

"Oh yeah."

"And?"

"And he's out."

Mark smiled, not believing things went as smoothly as his friend was making it sound. "He's out? You mean you guys just had a lovely little chat and agreed to part ways? Just like that?"

Cirella grinned. "Yeah, something like that."

"Interesting. It's not quite what I had anticipated."

"There might have been a few words said, a few punches thrown, a beer bottle being broken over someone's head, a girl getting thrown around, but it was pretty short."

"Sounds like a lively party." Mark took a look at the top of Cirella's head and didn't notice any bandages or cuts. "Doesn't seem like you got the worst end of it."

"Nah, I came out of it OK."

"Can the same be said for Danny?"

Cirella shrugged. "I guess it depends on your definition of OK. I mean, he's still breathing and all."

"I guess that's something."

"And probably more than he deserves."

"Well, just wanted to let you know that I've got feelers out there on the stuff you stole from Montgomery. Some promising stuff, but with the heat on, it's probably gonna take a month or two to get rid of it, and we're probably looking at the tail end of that estimate if not more."

"About what I figured."

"Yeah. I heard the police have some of their best detectives on the case, so hopefully the heat doesn't blow over on you."

"Should be fine," Cirella said. "We didn't leave any evidence behind. We're good."

"What about Danny?"

"What about him?"

"You fired him from the group. Think he might come at you for revenge? Do a little talking?"

"To the cops?" Cirella shook his head. "No, I don't think so. What's he gonna say? He'd go down for it as much as we would. He was there after all."

"He could negotiate a lesser charge just to watch you all go to the gas chamber."

"No, I don't see it. I could see him coming after all of us to try and kill us. But I can't picture him talking to the cops. Not unless he was already picked up for something else."

"Either way, it's something you're gonna have to keep an eye on," Mark said.

"If we start hearing chatter about it, then we'll resort to more drastic measures."

"I'll keep my ears open." Cirella nodded, content with how everything was going so far. "How 'bout Carter? Talk to him yet?"

"Not yet. Paid a few of his bills to create some good-will. Trying to slowly get him back in."

"You may have to work more quickly."

"Why?"

"May have another job coming up soon. Maybe a week or two."

"Any details?" Cirella asked.

"Would probably involve an armored car. Still working out the details and logistics, getting as much information as I can. Would definitely be a four-man job though, if not more. It would behoove you to get Carter on board as fast as you can."

"I'll ramp my efforts up."

"If not, I might have to give this to someone else. Or you'll have to get someone else you don't know as well."

"I'll talk to Carter tomorrow. I think I can swing him."

6

Carter was getting ready for work in the morning and was running a few minutes later than usual. He grabbed a cup of coffee and rushed out the door. Stacy stood at the door and gave him a kiss goodbye, holding Steven in her arms.

"Maybe we'll get more surprises today," Stacy said.

"I don't know if that's good or not."

"Have a good day."

Carter hopped in his car and quickly drove to the job site he was working on, getting there about five minutes before he was supposed to be there. His boss was OK if people got there a few minutes late, as long as it wasn't a habit, but Carter hated being late for anything. He had just gotten out of the car when he heard a familiar voice.

"Jack!"

Carter didn't move a muscle, knowing exactly who

the voice belonged to. It'd been a long time since he had heard it.

"What? You're not gonna say hello to an old friend?"

The voice was getting closer, and Carter finally turned around, seeing his old boss walking toward him. Cirella looked almost exactly the same as the last time they saw each other. It'd only been five years, but he'd aged well. The two men shook hands once they got close enough, though it was somewhat awkward and uncomfortable for Carter. They hadn't parted on bad terms, but it was still a little weird to be seeing Cirella after all this time.

"How's it going?" Cirella asked.

"Can't complain."

"Working construction now, huh?"

"Yeah. Nothing glamorous or anything, but it pays the bills. How'd you find me?"

"Oh, I just happened to be driving by and saw you. Figured I'd stop by and say hi."

"So, what are you up to these days?" Carter asked. "Still the same?"

Cirella smirked and shrugged. "Some things never change, right?"

"How are the rest of the boys?"

"They're good. They miss you. We all do."

"Yeah, maybe one day we can all go out for drinks or something."

"We should make that soon," Cirella said. "Boys would love to see you."

"So you working right now?"

"Between jobs at the moment."

"How's my replacement doing?"

"Ahh, not so good," Cirella answered. "We actually just kicked him to the curb. A little too rough around the edges for our tastes."

"That's too bad."

"Hey, you need a little extra money or anything? Could use you for some stuff coming up if you're interested."

Carter scratched his neck and kicked at the dirt. "Uhh, I dunno... I don't think so. I promised Stacy a long time ago that I was done with all that."

"Could be a really big payday. Might be talking a lot of money."

"Yeah, no, I don't think I'd be interested. I've got kids now. I really can't take that kind of risk."

"I understand. Why don't you think it over? If you change your mind, give me a call."

Cirella handed Carter a slip of paper with his phone number on it. Cirella then walked back to his car and drove away. He wasn't at all disappointed with how things turned out with Carter. He really didn't expect a yes right away. He knew it would likely take multiple conversations to get him back in the fold. He thought he saw some signs that Carter could be swayed over. Though Carter said no, he didn't say it in a strong, definitive way. Cirella figured he could convince him if he had enough time. Whether he could do it in time for the armored car job was another story. If not, they would likely have to pass on it.

For the rest of the day, Carter couldn't keep his mind off of seeing Cirella again. He really didn't believe it was just a coincidence that they ran into each other. He knew how Cirella worked, how he planned, how he schemed. He figured it was a calculated effort to talk to him again. Especially after hearing they got rid of his replacement. That meant that Cirella was there specifically to see him. He kept thinking about Cirella's offer and the chance of a big payday. Carter had to admit to himself that it was a tempting offer. He would never think about going back to the team full-time, not with a family and kids, but one or two jobs might be worth going back for, he thought. Maybe he would have to give Cirella more time to sell him and hear about the jobs first. Carter definitely wouldn't go back for anything he considered especially risky. But if there was a high probability of success, it was something he might have to think very strongly about.

By the time Carter got home from work, Stacy could see that something was weighing heavily on his mind. He seemed stressed out. And considering all their bills had been paid off for the month, she figured it couldn't have been that. At least not today.

"What is it?" Stacy asked.

Carter considered not talking to her about it and

keeping it to himself. But that was going to be hard to do. Especially if he eventually agreed to rejoin the crew for a job or two. That would require some time away from her and the kids. It would require some late-night outings, meetings, and planning. He didn't know how else he would explain his absence. Plus, he just didn't want to lie to her. He assumed she would eventually figure it out anyway. She was always good at that sort of thing. Carter reached into his pocket and removed the paper with Cirella's number on it. He looked at it for a moment, debating on whether to give it to her. After a few seconds, he handed it to her.

Stacy looked at it, unsure what she was looking at. "A phone number? What's it for? Who is it?"

"It's Dom."

"Dom?" Stacy asked, leaning her head forward slightly, making sure she understood properly. "Dom? As in Dominic? Dominic Cirella?"

Carter closed his eyes and nodded, almost not wanting to admit it. "Yeah."

"Uhh...." Stacy stuttered and stammered, seemingly stunned, unsure of what to say. And what was coming out of her mouth was not comprehensible.

"I know. I know."

"I don't understand. I don't understand what's going on here or what's happening. Why do you have his phone number?"

"He gave it to me today."

"He gave it to you? What? You saw him?"

"Yeah, he showed up at my job site as I got there. He just happened to be driving by."

Stacy laughed. "Just happened to be driving by. We've got a better chance of hitting the lottery than him happening to drive by your work. It's Dominic. We both know he planned that. That's how he is. Probably been following you."

"Maybe."

"So... what?" Stacy asked, demonstratively waving her arms in the air. "You guys are friends again?"

"He just gave me his number and said maybe we could go out for drinks sometime."

Stacy looked at him, distrust obvious in her eyes. She knew Cirella. He didn't do anything on a whim. Everything he did was calculated and planned. There were definitely no coincidences with him.

"He wants you to join up with him again?" Stacy asked. "Is that it?"

Jack shook his head. "We were just talking. Nothing more."

Stacy's face changed, like a light switch went off. "He's the one."

"What?"

"We were wondering who left the boxes of diapers, who paid off our bills... now we know. It was him."

"He didn't mention anything about that," Jack said.

"Of course he didn't. He wants something. He wants you."

"I told you I gave all that up a long time ago. Nothing's changed."

Stacy moved her jaw around, not happy with what she was thinking. "He's gonna keep coming after you until he pulls you back in. You know he will."

"It doesn't matter what he wants. I'm not going back."

"We both know he can be very convincing."

"It doesn't mean I have to do it."

"He's been checking up on us. He's doing that for a reason. It's not just out of the goodness of his heart. He saw that we've been struggling and is trying to buy his way in. Paying off our bills, giving us stuff for the kids... trying to create some goodwill for whatever he wants. He's trying to break you down so you'll eventually say yes to whatever he needs you for."

Jack hesitated in saying what he was about to but eventually let it come out. "Even if he does need me for something, maybe I should listen."

"What?"

"I mean, just because our bills are paid off for the month and we've got a few extra boxes of diapers doesn't mean we're out of the woods or anything. In a couple months we'll be right back in the same position we were before if we don't do something."

"I can keep looking for another job."

"But what if you can't find one?"

"I don't want you to go back to that life, Jack."

"I'm not saying I will or would. But maybe it's something to think about. Even if it's just for one job."

"And one job leads to two, and that leads to three, which leads to four, then before you know it, you're back to being a permanent member of the team."

"It doesn't have to," Jack said.

"Jack, let's not play games or kid each other here, OK? Even if you did just one job, are you really willing to roll the dice with your life?"

"What are you talking about?"

"Dom leads a professional crew. They don't just knock over the small drug dealer on a corner or rob little old ladies of their social security checks, they're a big-time crew, that takes big-time risks, and puts themselves in some high-risk situations. So don't pretend that you're not taking a chance with your life every time you do a job with them."

"Don't overdramatize it."

"Are you really prepared to make your wife a widow and your children fatherless?"

"Stacy..."

"Don't Stacy me. You know full well that that's a distinct possibility."

"Nobody on that crew has ever gotten killed," Jack replied, trying to ease her mind, not that he had much of a chance of succeeding.

"Oh, great, so you'll just go to jail then. And don't tell me that's not a possibility because I know damn well that the other three were sent to prison."

Jack sighed, knowing there was nothing he could say that would ease her mind any. And he wasn't sure why he was even trying. He wasn't even sure if it was something he was planning on doing. But he thought he owed it to his family to explore every possibility that would get them out of their financial difficulties. Not wanting to talk about it any longer and risk getting into a fight with his wife over it, Carter grabbed Stacy by the waist and pulled her closer to him. He hugged her, wishing they could escape all their troubles and leave them behind. Unfortunately, life just didn't work that way. And he knew Stacy was correct in her assessment of Cirella. He'd be coming again for him. Carter just had to hope he'd be strong enough to resist.

7

A couple of days had passed since Cirella's first meeting with Carter. Cirella wanted to give him some time to think about everything before approaching him again. In the meantime, Cirella had been called to Mark's house for another meeting to go over the armored car information. He had some new details.

"Before we get into the job, how's things with Carter?" Mark asked. "Work him over yet?"

"Uhh, yeah, you know, I talked to him for a few minutes the other day, just trying to work back into things. Told him I might have another job coming up, but I didn't get too heavy into anything. Don't want to overwhelm him with everything right off the bat. Just wanted to plant some seeds."

"Well, you better hope that tree sprouts quickly

and produces some fruit in the next day or two otherwise I don't know how you're gonna do this."

"Why? You got more specifics?"

"I do," Mark answered. "And you're gonna need him if you get this job."

"How much we talking?"

"Score's gonna be right around a million. That's gonna have to be split six, seven, eight ways."

"Why so many?"

"Well, there's your four, plus me, plus my contact, then probably two other guys if we do it the way I'm thinking."

"You want me to take two more guys I don't know and put them on my crew?" Cirella asked, not quite liking the arrangement.

Mark knew he'd object to that part and sought to ease his mind. "They wouldn't have to exactly be with you. They don't even need a gun in their hands."

"Then what would I need them for?"

"Blocking traffic."

"Blocking traffic?"

"Here's what I'm thinking," Mark said, putting some paper down on the table between them. "This armored car, after getting a pickup, will have to go down this stretch of road." Mark drew a long street, putting an x on both sides of the street to indicate a bunch of trees that lined the road. He also drew intersections at the far ends of the street to show where he'd want the traffic blocked. "Now if we block traffic immediately after that armored car comes through here, and we already have the traffic blocked on the far end, to where they're going, we have a completely wide-open stretch of road to work with. Don't have to worry about bystanders, or cars coming through, or being interrupted, anything. It's wide open."

"How would we hit it then?"

"Right here in the middle, there's a small unpaved road." Mark hastily drew a couple of lines to indicate the location of the dirt road. "Just leads to a small water station. I've already checked, and there should be nobody there at that time of day when the truck will be coming through. No maintenance or anything."

Cirella then pointed to the unpaved road. "If we sit on this road here, are we going to be able to see the car coming?"

"Should be able to, yes."

Cirella intently stared at the paper, putting his hand over his mouth, rubbing his cheek and chin as he tried to come up with a plan. "We could have two trucks there. We could have a big rig, or a semi, waiting there. The other three of us would be in our regular car. Then when the armored car comes, we ram it with the semi, knocking it off the road, make them disoriented, then the other car comes in, blows the back door off."

"Sounds good. The whole thing wouldn't even take that long. You could be in and out in just a few minutes. You know, I could get four guys to block traffic, two on each side, pay them twenty thousand each and call it a day."

"Reliable?" Cirella asked, always concerned about trusting people he didn't know. They would have to trust that these people would do their job and hold off any traffic from interfering. Cirella wouldn't be able to stay with them and hold their hand to make sure they were doing things right.

"I'll make good on it, don't worry. I'll make sure they're trustworthy. If there's even a doubt, I won't hire them."

"You think they'll do it for twenty gees?"

Mark grinned. "Think about it. All you gotta do is stand there and stop traffic for ten minutes. Do that and you collect twenty thousand. Wouldn't you?"

Cirella laughed. "Yeah. I guess I would."

"Twenty thousand to stand there for ten minutes. I mean, that's more than Joe Schmoe makes working twenty hours a week in one of those department stores, right?"

"Yeah."

"Not a bad haul for ten minutes. All this depends on you, though."

"What do you mean?"

"On whether you think you can get Carter in the fold. Or I find someone else to put on your team. Or you think you can pull it off with just the three of you."

Cirella grimaced. He wasn't crazy about operating

shorthanded. "We could probably do it with three, but four would make me a lot more comfortable."

"Me too."

"Especially if something goes sideways: we don't hit the car just right, the guards put up a fight, we end up in a firefight. An extra guy there would be helpful."

"I agree. That's why I want you to have the job. You're the most dependable, but with only three men, I dunno. You want me to start working some people and see if I can get someone for you?"

"How much time we working with?"

"We got one week from today," Mark said. "But you'll probably want a few days to go over the route, prepare, plan, make sure everyone's on the same page. That would mean you only got two or three days at most to bring him back in."

"Guess I'll have to work more quickly then."

CIRELLA DIDN'T WASTE any more time in trying to court Carter again. After leaving Mark's, he went directly over to Carter's house. If Cirella wanted this job, and he did, he couldn't afford to waste time. He had to dive right in and hope he pulled up gold. He got to Carter's house a little after seven, giving the family enough time to eat dinner before he interrupted them. He parked in front of the house and called Rollins to let him know he was about to make a better pitch to their former colleague.

"You think it's wise to go after him so hard already?" Rollins asked.

"We don't have any other choice. If we don't bring him on board, we do this job short-handed, or with some slob we don't know that Mark brings on. I don't know about you, but I don't feel all that good about working with someone on a job like this that I've never met before."

"Yeah, I agree with you there."

"I'll just lay it on the line and let him know how much money's at stake," Cirella said. "I mean, they've been having money problems for a while, it could be enough to sway him."

"What if me and Isaac come over? We can hit him up as a team. Try to get him thinking about the old times and all?"

"Nah, I don't think that'd be wise. Especially at his house, with his wife there, he might think we're ganging up on him, and he might just clam up. Especially Stacy, she's gonna be a big obstacle to overcome. All of us being there will just make it worse."

"All right. Hope you can pull it off."

Cirella hung up and then got out of the car to walk up the asphalt driveway. He kept his eyes peeled on the window to see if they saw him coming. He didn't notice anything though. He went up to the door and knocked, hearing the television on inside. He heard someone coming to the door and hoped it was Carter. Not that he had anything against Stacy. He liked her personally, but he knew how she felt about him. He didn't think Stacy disliked him personally, but he knew she didn't approve of their lifestyle.

Cirella's hopes were dashed, though, when he saw Stacy's pretty face when the door opened. She looked stunned to see him standing there. While Cirella immediately gave her a smile, Stacy wasn't quite as willing or able to reciprocate the gesture. Truth be told, she was just too surprised to give much of any kind of reaction.

"Stacy... still looking as beautiful as ever."

Stacy finally smiled, though she wasn't falling for his smooth-talking ways. She was much too smart for that. "Dominic... hi."

"Mind if I come in?"

Stacy opened her mouth to say something but suddenly stopped. She then let out a deep breath. "Why?"

Cirella shrugged. "Uhh, I dunno, just wanted to talk to Jack. See how you guys were doing. It's been a long time."

"I mean, why are you here? Really?"

"Nothing more than that."

Stacy let out a fake laugh, knowing that couldn't be further from the truth. "Dom, this isn't the first time we've met or talked."

Cirella put his hand up as if he was being sworn

onto the witness stand at a trial. "I swear, I have nothing else on my mind, no evil intentions. Just wanna talk. Not trying to pressure anybody into anything."

Stacy still wasn't buying what he was selling. And before she allowed him to do anything, she wanted some answers that she wasn't sure she'd get from her husband, whether he actually knew them or not.

"So are you the one who sent the diapers and formula the other day?"

Cirella looked down with a smug smile on his face, then threw both arms up to each of his sides. "Guilty."

"Why?"

"I got word that you guys were struggling. Just wanted to help."

"You got word we were struggling? From whom?"

"Uhh, you know, I don't quite remember," Cirella said, not wanting to admit he was actually digging into their life.

Stacy briefly looked away and rolled her eyes, knowing he was giving her a canned line. "One other thing, you wouldn't happen to know how all of our bills got paid off for this month, do you?"

Cirella wasn't going to lie. He might stretch the truth a little, but he knew Stacy had her bullshit antennas up and was waiting for him to trip up some- where. He wasn't going to fall for that. He knew it was best to just be as honest as possible with her, at least as much as he could be without admitting he was actively trying to recruit her husband again.

"Guilty again," Cirella admitted. "It was me."

"Why are you doing all this? Really?"

"Honestly, Stacy, it's nothing more than just trying to help out a former member of my crew who's fallen on some hard times. I've got some extra money, you guys could use some, I just figured I'd do the decent thing and try to help."

Stacy looked like she still didn't buy it. "So you're telling me you just did all that out of the goodness of your heart?"

"Why else would I?"

"Maybe because you need Jack for something?"

"I swear to you, on my mother's grave, that I do not have any kind of ulterior motives in helping out or being here. Nothing at all. Just trying to do a good deed and all that."

"Excuse me for being skeptical, but nobody would ever accuse you of being a saint."

"That's true, and I would never even try to pretend I was, but there's nothing nefarious about me being here. But in being honest, as I try to be, if Jack were to come up to me and say he wanted back in, I probably wouldn't stand in his way. He's always been a good guy and one of my favorite people, but this is not about me trying to recruit him again. I've always respected his wishes and wouldn't go against whatever he wanted."

"Uh huh."

"Remember, I let him out of the group before without putting up a stink. I could've put up a fight to keep him, but I didn't. He wanted to make a life with you and I always respected that."

"I recall a prison sentence might have had something to do with that."

Cirella grinned, thinking she'd have made a good investigator or attorney. "Stacy, I swear, I just came here to talk to you guys and make sure you were doing OK. If you guys need more help or anything, I just wanted to let you know you can always come to me. If you need anything, all you have to do is ask."

"And what would it cost us?" Stacy cynically asked.

"Nothing. Absolutely nothing. I'm not some kind of bank or anything. Nothing needs to be paid back or anything. Everything's on the up-and-up."

"So you're not looking for anything in return for the bills being paid and the diapers and all?"

"Absolutely not," Cirella replied, wiping his hands clean. "We're square all the way through."

Though she still didn't trust him, Stacy really didn't want to stand there talking to him all night either. She knew he was really there to see Jack. And while she didn't want them talking alone, because she knew Cirella was going to do something to try to lure her husband back in, she also didn't want Cirella in her house and around her children. She also wasn't going to make Jack's decisions for him. She was just going to have to hope that he had the good sense to see through Cirella's facade.

"Wait here," Stacy said. "I'll get Jack."

Stacy closed the door, then went into the living room where Jack was sitting down on the floor, playing with the kids.

"Who was it?" Jack asked.

"I'll bet you don't even need two guesses."

"Huh?"

"Well, there's someone outside waiting for you."

"There is? Who?"

Stacy gave him a look, like he really didn't need to ask. "Guess."

Jack hesitated for a second, having a good idea who it was, mostly from Stacy's bristled demeanor. "Dominic?"

Stacy let out a false laugh. "See? Told you you wouldn't need two guesses."

"What's he want?"

"What do you think he wants? You."

"But why?"

"I don't know. He says he came by to talk and see how we were doing. Oh yeah, and by the way, he admitted to being the one who dropped off the diapers and paid our bills."

"He did?"

"Yes. I asked him and he said he did."

"Why?"

"He said he heard we were struggling and he just wanted to help us out."

Jack could tell by the sarcastic tone in her voice that she didn't believe any of that. "Guess I should go talk to him, huh?"

"I guess."

The two of them then traded positions, with Stacy settling down on the floor, and Jack walking towards the front door. Stacy watched as he walked away, keeping an eye on him as he opened the door and stepped outside, closing the door behind him. She hoped he didn't do anything stupid.

"Hey," Carter said, upon seeing his former leader standing there. "What are you doing here?"

"Just wanted to talk some more, see how you were."

"We're good."

"Really? That's not what I hear."

"No, we're good."

"Been having some financial problems?" Cirella asked.

"Nothing we can't handle. I guess every family struggles with money at some point along the way. We'll get by."

"You will. You're a fighter, and I know you guys will manage."

"Stacy told me you paid our bills, dropped off diapers and stuff. Guess I should say thank you."

Cirella waved his hand at him. "Ahh, happy to do it."

"How'd you know how to do all that? How'd you know we were behind on bills?"

Cirella shrugged. "Sometimes you just get lucky, run into the right people. Anyway, that's not important. What is important is that you guys got a little relief right now."

"Well, we appreciate it. Hopefully it doesn't put you in a hole or anything."

"Ahh, don't worry about me. I'm not hurting."

"Still doing the apartment thing and living the single life?"

Cirella smiled. "You know me. Can't get tied down yet. Not until all this is over. No complications, no distractions, no excuses."

"Still got that five million mark in mind?"

"Yeah, you know, still striving for it. I figure when I hit that number, then I'm out. Then I know I can live comfortably for the rest of my life."

"How close are you?"

"Uhh, still got a few million more to go," Cirella said with a laugh. "That little prison stretch put a serious hold on things."

Carter looked down, a little embarrassed that every member of the team got sent to prison except for him. When they got picked up, Carter wasn't with them, but they could've put the finger on him to lessen their own sentences. But none of them did. To a man, they all said they were only a three-man crew, even when presented with evidence that the police knew there was a fourth man. Carter always felt bad about that, feeling like he should've got sent up with the rest of the team. It took him a while to shed the guilty feeling for getting away, but seeing Cirella again was starting to bring back some of those feelings.

"Umm, about all that," Carter said, trying to think of the right words to express his gratitude for never getting sent to prison with the rest of them, "I guess I just… thanks for never saying anything about me."

Cirella smiled and put his hand behind Carter's neck in a friendly manner. "That's not how we do business, you know that. You were always a good guy, you were one of us, we were always glad you didn't wind up like the rest of us. You deserved to get away, start a new life."

"A lot of good it did me. Wind up having to get bailed out…" Carter didn't finish his thought, not wanting to sound down and depressed about his current financial status.

Cirella could see he was a little upset thinking about it and wanted to change the subject. "Hey, that's all behind us now, right? We're looking forward, not back."

Carter took a deep breath, not sure if he really wanted to ask his next question, fearful of the answer, as well as his own reply. "Dom, why are you here?"

"What do you mean?"

"I mean, all of this, everything. Bumping into me at

work, the diapers, the paying off the bills, everything. It's not all just a coincidence or wanting to help, is it?"

Cirella looked at him, a grin on his face, knowing his charade wasn't working. Maybe it was all for the best. Maybe it was better if he just came out with it and stopped messing around.

"OK. OK, you're right, I'm not just here playing Santa Claus and all. We're down a man right now, like I mentioned before, and time's running short, and we need someone to step in."

"And you want me?"

"Your name has come up."

"I've been out of the game a long time now. I mean, five, six years, might as well be twenty."

"It's like riding a bike. Once you know how you never forget. Maybe the skills just need to be sharpened a bit, but they're still there."

"Why not just get someone else who's still involved?"

"Because we know you," Cirella answered. "We trust you, like you... we know we can depend on you. In this business, that's critical, and probably more important than anything else. I'd rather have someone I know and trust instead of someone I don't know who comes recommended."

"Still doing business with Mark?"

Cirella smiled. "Yeah, he's still around and kicking."

Carter put his hand on the back of his head and rubbed his neck as he thought about things. He promised Stacy he was done with all that, and it was important to him to keep that promise. But he made that promise long before he had two kids that he now had to worry about. Their health and well-being superseded anything else. Plus, with the money problems they'd been having lately, a little extra would sure go a long way.

Cirella could see the anguish on Carter's face as he thought. He knew he was close to getting a yes. "This doesn't have to be a long-term thing. I know you got a wife and kids now, and I'm happy for you for that, and if you don't wanna do this long-term, believe me, I get it. But if you wanna hang around for a job or two, you can make a little extra money, put you and your family in a really good financial spot. Set yourself up for a long time."

"I dunno, Dom. What kind of jobs are we talking?"

"Before we get into all that, we're working in a very tight window right now, so we don't have a lot of time to wait for an answer. Believe me, in a perfect world, I could give you all the time you wanted, as much as you need, days, weeks, months, whatever. Unfortunately, I don't have that kind of time. We've got a job lined up for next week, and I'm gonna need an answer pretty quickly."

"I don't know if I can give you an answer right now."

"Let me tell you about this job first," Cirella said. "Maybe that'll help make up your mind."

"OK?"

"We got an armored car job. Pretty good setup."

"Armored cars aren't easy."

"This one's good. It's gonna be travelling a long stretch of road, trees all around, isolated, we're gonna have both ends of the street blocked off, so we're not gonna have to worry about traffic, bystanders, none of that. Somewhere around the middle, there's an unpaved road that goes off to the side where we'll be waiting with a semi and our regular truck. When the armored car reaches that road, we'll ram it with the semi."

"Doesn't sound too bad," Carter said, growing more intrigued by the minute.

"If you want to get back in with a job that doesn't have a lot of risks, this is it. As long as whoever Mark gets to block the streets upholds their end of the bargain, we should have a clear path."

"And if they don't?"

"Then we'll have to go to work. I mean, those guards in the truck might give us a problem too, but with all four of us, I'm not worried about that. The only thing I'm worried about is the streets being blocked. The actual job part, we can handle that."

Carter puffed his cheeks out, then blew air through his mouth, the decision he'd have to make tantalizing him. No matter what Cirella said, it was a risk. Carter knew that. There was no such thing as an easy job. You always had to anticipate something going wrong. It came down to whether Carter believed it was an acceptable risk. And he wasn't sure he knew that yet. This could have been a life changing decision, and it wasn't one he believed he could make on the spot. He needed time.

"I just don't know if I can make a decision right now," Carter said.

Cirella nodded. "I understand. How 'bout tomorrow? I'm really not sure I can hold off any longer than that."

"Uhh, yeah, yeah, I guess tomorrow would work."

"How 'bout we do this? Take tonight, take all day tomorrow, let's meet for dinner tomorrow night and you give me your answer. Even if you decide to turn it down, I'll understand. We meet for dinner, we'll talk it over, I'll bring the boys, we can discuss things, options, whatever, and then you make the call. You decide it's not right for you, I'll accept your decision and we'll move on. You go back to the wife and kids, I'll look for someone else. What do you say?"

Carter and Cirella then shook hands, agreeing to postpone his decision for a day. "I'd say that sounds like a deal."

8

As the day went on, Carter still wasn't sure what he was going to do. The prospect of a big payday was really gnawing at him, making him think he should give it a go, even though he knew Stacy wouldn't like it. He mentioned something in passing to her before he left for work, but Jack knew a bigger discussion would be coming later before he left to meet his old buddies. He didn't want to put his family at risk of having him locked up or dead, but if Cirella was right, and the job had minimal risks, it may have been worth it. He debated, went back and forth, changed his mind constantly throughout the day, flip-flopping on what he really wanted. By the time he got home from work that hadn't changed. He still did not have a definitive answer. Stacy was in the kitchen making dinner.

"Dinner will be ready in about twenty minutes," she said.

"I'll just skip it. I was meeting Dominic and the guys anyway."

Stacy sighed and continued getting dinner ready, not even looking at her husband so he could see the disappointment on her face, even though he could tell that she was.

"I haven't agreed to anything," Jack said. "Just talking."

"The fact that it's even gotten this far makes it pretty easy to determine what you're thinking."

"I just... I feel like I owe it to us to at least listen to what he has to say."

"You owe it to us?" Stacy asked, finally turning around to look at him. "Really? Don't you owe it to us to actually be around and not rotting in some prison cell?"

"Stacy, you're only looking at it one way."

"And you're only looking at it from the other. You think all the other people in jail actually thought they were going to be caught?"

"If I agree to do this, and I said if, I mean, we're talking about enough money that we don't have to worry and struggle for the next few years."

"Jack, I get it, the prospect of having more money is really enticing, and I understand that, but is it really worth risking being pulled away from your family? I can keep looking for another job, maybe you get a second job, we can still do this the right way."

"Yeah, we both work our fingers to the bone, not seeing each other or our kids because we're always away working. I don't know about you, but I don't really want to have to work two jobs, sixty or seventy hours a week. How 'bout you? If I'm never here because I'm working, the kids still won't see me and neither will you. So how would that be any different?"

"Because you wouldn't be in jail and you'd be safe," Stacy replied. "It wouldn't have to be forever. Just until we get things sorted out."

"And how long will that take? A few years? What if it never does? Some people struggle their entire lives you know."

The more Jack was talking, the more he realized he seemed to be convincing himself of what he wanted to do. Everything he was saying had him leaning towards working with Cirella again. He knew Stacy wouldn't like it, but he had to do what he felt was best for his family. He had to hope that eventually she'd accept his decision.

"I gotta get ready," Jack said, leaving the kitchen to get changed out of his work clothes.

After getting dressed, Jack went back into the kitchen and told his wife that he was leaving to meet the old crew. He kissed the kids, then came around to Stacy, who kept her head turned, only letting Jack kiss her cheek. He knew he was going to get the cold shoulder from her. He just had to hope that it wouldn't last too long. He then left the house, seemingly content with the decision that he thought he was going to make.

CIRELLA, Rollins, and Brantly were already at the restaurant, waiting for their guest to arrive. It was a family type restaurant, booths around the perimeter of the building, with a sports bar in the middle. They'd taken up one of the booths, wanting a little more privacy than talking out in the open at the bar area. They were excited, hoping their old friend was going to hook up with them again.

"What do you think?" Rollins asked. "You think he's coming?"

"He said he'd be here," Cirella answered. "I have no doubt he will."

"No, but will he jump back in with us?"

Cirella shrugged. "Tough to say."

"You seem to be taking this all in stride."

"What are you gonna do? It's not our decision. All we can do is lay it on the line, tell it like it is, tell him what's at stake, and hope for the best. Hope that he makes an informed decision and falls back in."

"What's your gut say?" Brantly asked.

"My gut says I'm hungry. Hope he gets here soon so we can start eating."

The three men shared a laugh, looking around at the crowd. The building was only about half full at the moment; it wouldn't get busy for another hour or so.

"I hope he comes back in," Brantly said.

"Even if he does," Rollins said, "he might not be the same guy as before. Having a wife and kids can change a person. Maybe he's softer. Maybe he's not willing to do what needs to be done"

"Maybe so," Cirella said. "But we're also not walking into a street fight either. All we need him to do is hold down the perimeter while we take care of the armored car."

"I hope so."

"You want me to call Danny back and tell him no hard feelings, you're back in the group?"

Rollins shook his head. "No. I'm good with this."

"Jack will be fine. Even if you're out of the game for a while, doesn't mean anything. I did three years in prison; did it do anything to me?"

"Yeah, but you're not married or have kids. I'm telling you, some guys change their perspective, start thinking about them while they're on the job instead of focusing on the job. It can happen."

"We'll see."

"So, what's your gut say?" Brantly asked. "Besides that you're hungry. How'd Jack seem when you talked to him about this?"

"He seemed interested but unsure. I'm sure he had his family in mind, like Noah says, but I think his financial issues were weighing on him. That's just me reading his face and all, but I think he's going to come back in. Even if it's just for a job or two to get him out of his current situation. I think he'll be good to go."

About ten minutes went by with still no sign of Carter. Though the others were starting to worry a little, Cirella wasn't nervous in the least. He knew Carter would be there. He looked at the time. Carter was only a minute or two late. No need to worry yet. Cirella wouldn't change his tune unless another half hour went by. And even if it did, he knew where Carter lived.

"I hope he shows up soon, I'm getting hungry too," Rollins said. "I feel like my stomach's about to eat itself."

"Let's order an appetizer first to hold us over," Brantly said.

After calling a waitress over and ordering an appetizer, they finally saw Carter entering the building.

"He's here," Rollins said, looking at their old friend.

The other two looked over their booth towards the entrance, all of them locking eyes on Carter. Carter initially didn't see them, looking around the restaurant. Once he finally did, Rollins and Brantly waved him over. As Carter walked over to the table, knots filled his stomach. It'd been a long time since he'd seen them. They'd always gotten along very well, almost like brothers, but time changed people. He knew it changed him. What if they weren't like they were before? What if prison hardened them? It didn't seem to change Cirella much, but he was a special case, he always had the same view no matter what. Carter wasn't so sure about the others.

As Carter approached the table, Brantly was so excited at seeing his friend that he lunged at him, giving him a big bear hug. Carter couldn't help but smile, patting Brantly on the back.

"OK, man, OK," Carter said. "Don't wanna break my ribs now."

"So good to see you, man."

"You too, bud, you too."

When Brantly finally relinquished his grip on Carter, Rollins walked over to him and did the same, though his bear hug wasn't quite as strong. Carter felt like he could still breathe with his.

"Been a long time, man," Rollins said, letting go and rubbing the top of Carter's head. "Too long."

"I know."

Carter then looked at Cirella, who was still sitting, and nodded, greeting him with a handshake again.

"Sit down," Cirella said. "We just ordered some appetizers."

"Good, I'm hungry," Carter replied.

"You ain't the only one," Rollins said.

Carter sat across from Cirella, Brantly sitting next to him, with Rollins sitting next to their leader. Much to Carter's surprise, they didn't say a thing to him about joining the group again, at least not at first. The appetizers came a few minutes later, which they all enjoyed, and they ordered their main dishes. For the next hour, they talked about almost everything, their lives, time in prison, what they'd been doing since they got out, Carter's family, everything but what they were really there to discuss.

It was actually part of Cirella's strategy, not that he shared it with the others, but he wanted to remind Carter how close they all were at some point. If Carter was having any doubts prior to their meeting, Cirella hoped reminiscing would help to sway him back toward them. By the way they were all interacting with each other, it seemed to be working. They were all laughing and having a good time. It was almost like they'd never been apart. Even Carter's nervousness had gone away. Everyone was exactly the same as the last time he saw them. Nobody seemed to have changed. Nobody except for him that is. And it wasn't that he was really different, at least not his personality, because he was pretty much the same guy he always was. But he was the only one whose life had changed.

After the hour went by, Cirella figured it was time to get down to business. There was only so long he could postpone it or try to rope Carter back in. Now it was time to make a decision. They needed an answer one way or another so they could either start preparing or move on. Cirella pushed his empty plate to the side as he began talking.

"As much as I hate to stop reminiscing and thinking about all the good times we've had, I think it's time we get down to the nitty gritty here."

"Yeah, I guess so," Carter replied.

"Before we do anything, let me map out everything so we can visualize it better."

Cirella grabbed a napkin and took out a pen, then started to draw everything. After he was done, he turned it around so Carter could see what he was saying, which was exactly what he told him the day before. Carter studied the drawing for a minute or two. It was how he pictured it from what Cirella told him back at the house.

"So, what do you think?" Cirella asked.

"I mean, it looks like a good plan," Carter answered.

"Something you might be interested in?"

Carter wiped his forehead, thinking of his options. Of course, he only had two of them. One was to jump in and definitely anger or alienate his wife, the other was to decline and go back to the same hopeless situation he was already in. The second option didn't appeal to him at all. And if doing this pissed off his wife, well, he'd just have to hope she stuck with him and that he could eventually make it up to her.

"What kind of payout are we talking?" Carter asked, ready to be convinced.

"Low end is probably a hundred grand," Cirella replied. "Could be more depending on other factors, but a hundred is almost guaranteed. Could be as much as a hundred and fifty. Tough to say right now. Mark gets his cut, he's gotta pay some inside guys for the information, plus the guys blocking both ends of the street will get their cut, but that shouldn't amount to more than fifty thousand combined for them."

"A hundred thousand's gotta look pretty good right now," Rollins said, trying to do his part in convincing his ex-partner.

Carter nodded. "It does." It was hard to walk away from that kind of money. Especially when it looked like such a good plan, without a high degree of risk. It might have been different if they were walking into a bank or some other business that had a lot of safe-guards in place. But this seemed pretty low on the risk factor. Assuming the streets were blocked off, all they had to worry about was the guards.

"What do you think?" Cirella asked.

"What would my role be?"

"You'd be the lookout. Isaac's gonna drive the semi, so he'll ram the car. Us three will be in the SUV. You'll drive, so me and Noah can quickly jump out to pounce. Us three will approach the armored car. We'll take out the guards if necessary. We'll open the door. We'll do all that. What we need from you is to watch our back just in case something doesn't go according to plan."

"Like somebody getting past the roadblock?"

"Exactly."

"But we need to make sure you're ready to do what's necessary if it comes to that," Rollins said.

"I don't wanna kill anybody," Carter said.

"I'm not asking you to," Cirella said. "I don't wanna kill anybody either. And I won't unless my life is threatened. And I wouldn't expect anything different out of you. Just do what's necessary. Keep your eyes peeled. If anyone gets past the roadblock, if they're innocent, scare them off. If they're a threat, keep them busy until we can get out of there. We're the same crew we've always been. We just do what's necessary to survive. Nothing more than that."

"C'mon, man," Brantly said. "Hundred thousand's gotta really help you out now."

"It would," Carter said.

"What do you say?" Cirella asked.

Carter took another look down at the napkin, analyzing the plan for another minute. He then lifted his head up and looked at each of the three men at the table, all of whom seemed to be eagerly hanging on his decision.

"I say... I'm in."

Cirella finally let a small grin creep over his face while Rollins and Brantly clapped their hands and pumped their fists into the air. The group then gave each other high-fives, happy to have the band back together again. It was a day none of them could ever envision happening. Cirella and Carter shook hands again.

"Good to have you back in the fold," Cirella said. "You won't regret it."

Carter's mind immediately went to Stacy, knowing how disappointed she'd be right now. "I hope not."

9

After spending another hour in the restaurant, the team finished up, paid their bill, and went outside. The four men were standing by Cirella's car talking, letting Carter know what their plans were for the next couple of days. Suddenly, a shot rang out. All four men instinctively squatted as the driver's side window to Cirella's car shattered, pieces crashing down to the ground.

"What the hell was that?" Rollins asked.

"Who's shooting at us?" Brantly said.

Cirella rose up, not seemingly caring whether any more bullets were headed in their direction. He looked across the street and saw a black sports car spinning its wheels as it took off after sitting along the curb. Cirella's cheeks puffed out in anger, knowing exactly who was shooting at them. Rollins noticed the car pulling out as well and stood next to his boss.

"Is that who I think it is?" Rollins asked.

"Yeah."

"Damn fool."

"Let's go," Cirella said, hurrying to get into his truck. Rollins jumped into the front passenger seat, while Brantly hopped in the back. Carter took a few steps back, not knowing exactly what was going on. Cirella turned to him, looking out his newly broken window. "I'll call you tomorrow."

"What's going on?" Carter asked.

"Just some idiot who doesn't know when to leave well enough alone. Don't worry about it."

Cirella then quickly backed up and sped off, zooming out of the parking lot and onto the main street, driving fast to try to catch up with their former teammate. Cirella immediately recognized Falk's black sports car. He had custom wheels put on it which was a dead giveaway.

"What's he doing?" Rollins asked.

"Apparently he's got a death wish," Cirella answered. "Damn idiot. Doesn't know when to just let it go."

"Guess he had a problem with being fired," Brantly said.

"Either that or the part where I worked him over."

"Didn't he come after you?"

"Yeah, but I'm sure that doesn't matter much to him."

"Wherever he's going, it's not to his apartment," Rollins said. "That's in the other direction."

"Doesn't matter," Cirella replied. "I'll follow him wherever he's going."

"What are we gonna do when we catch up to him?"

"Probably what I should have done before. I gave him the benefit of the doubt, but not now. Not anymore. Now he's a dead man. Nobody takes a shot at us and gets away with it."

"What's he even thinking?"

"That's most of his problem. He doesn't think. He just reacts without thinking of the repercussions and complications."

They drove for a few more minutes, still seeing the taillights to Falk's sports car up ahead, zooming in and out of traffic, trying to stay ahead of his pursuers. Cirella put his foot on the gas, trying to catch up with him. He started to inch closer. A red light popped up that Falk completely blew through, causing a few cars to lay on their horns. Cirella wasn't going to be stopped either. He slowed as he cruised through the intersection, blasting his horn so no one would plow into him, making the other cars come to a standstill. Once Cirella successfully navigated his way through, he almost put his foot through the floor in order to ramp his car up again.

"Look, he's still up there," Rollins said, pointing to Falk's car ahead of them.

"It looked like he was slowing down," Brantly said.

"What's he up to? He couldn't have possibly hoped to take us all out back there, could he?"

"Who knows what's going through that head of his," Cirella said.

The two cars continued flying down the highway, Cirella seemingly gaining on his target with each passing minute. Falk eventually made a couple turns to go in a different direction.

"Where's he going?" Brantly asked.

"I don't think he knows," Rollins answered. "I think he's just going. Driving aimlessly."

"No, I think he's got a plan," Cirella said.

"What is it?"

"I don't know. Something's not feeling right."

"Wanna break it off?"

"We'll keep it going a few more minutes."

The more Cirella thought about it, the more concerned he was getting. Rollins was right, Falk couldn't have reasonably expected to take them all out back at the restaurant. Maybe Falk was just trying to take out his former leader, but Cirella didn't think so. Everything about the situation seemed to suggest that Falk wanted them to know it was him and follow him. Falk had a faster car, so he could've pulled away from them anytime he wanted to, but he didn't. He was making it appear like he was trying to get away, but it seemed to Cirella like he was trying to go just fast enough to allow his former crew to keep up with him.

A few more minutes went by as the chase

continued until they reached the train yard. There must have been a hundred train cars sitting there, some abandoned, never to be used again, some just waiting for their next job. As Cirella pulled up to the yard, they observed Falk's car sitting idle by the fence, the driver's side door open. On instinct, the three men would have jumped out of the car, but Cirella's feeling had now spread to the other two. The three of them just sat there, motionless, staring at the car. Cirella then tapped Rollins on the leg and motioned to the glove box. Rollins opened it and removed three hand-guns, keeping one for himself, and passing the others to his partners.

Cirella partially opened his door. "Stay sharp."

"Wait a minute," Rollins said, looking around through his window. "I got a bad feeling about this."

"You're not the only one."

"Maybe we should pull back. Let it slide."

"If we do, we'll just have to deal with him another time."

"I don't like this, Dom. This don't feel right."

"I know it."

"What if he was just trying to draw us all here so he could pick us off?"

"Possible," Cirella said.

Cirella fully exited the car with Brantly doing the same. Rollins sat there an extra minute, not really wanting to proceed. He had a feeling that more than just Falk was out there. As Cirella and Brantly approached Falk's car, their arms extended in front of them, their guns pointed at the vehicle in case anything jumped out at them, Rollins finally got out of the car as well. Cirella cautiously approached the driver's side, as Brantly did the same to the passenger's side, while Rollins approached the rear. It was empty. The three men looked around, with Rollins eventually noticing an open gate about fifty feet away from them. He tapped Cirella on the arm and pointed out the gate to him. The three men turned around and looked through the metal fencing.

"What do you wanna do?" Rollins asked.

Cirella thought about it for a second, knowing that Falk had likely set something special up for them. "Let's go in."

"Dom, this has all the makings of an ambush."

"I know."

"There's no telling how many people he's got in there. He's probably not alone."

"Well, then let's get it over with."

Rollins was certainly no coward and didn't have a problem with difficult situations, but the fear of the unknown was getting to him in this situation. He liked knowing what the odds were in any fight he got into. And he didn't like walking into something where he thought the deck was stacked against him. That's what this felt like to him.

"Wouldn't it be better to just let this ride for another time?"

"I know what you're saying," Cirella replied. "And I don't think you're wrong. But if we let this go now, all we're doing is giving him another chance to get us later. And who knows when and where that would be? Maybe we'd be in an even tougher spot next time. I mean, he's certainly going to try this again. At least right now, we know where he is. Next time, who knows? And I really don't wanna be looking over my shoulder for the next few weeks or months wondering where he's gonna show up next, do you?"

Rollins sighed, understanding Cirella's point. Not that he necessarily liked it, but he understood and knew where he was coming from and couldn't really disagree with his point of view.

"Yeah, I guess."

"If you'd rather not, stay here and watch our backs," Cirella said

Cirella and Brantly started walking for the opened gate as Rollins just stood there. Rollins took a deep breath, then shook his head, not liking this situation one bit. As much as he didn't want to proceed, he wasn't about to just let his friends go in there without him. He shuffled his feet, then started walking toward the others. Cirella looked back, watching Rollins jog their way, glad that he was joining them. As they walked through the gate, they looked at their surroundings, trying to come up with a plan.

"What do you wanna do?" Brantly asked. "Split up?"

"No, that's a fool's game," Cirella answered. "That's what they probably want us to do. Divide and conquer. We're better off sticking together that way they can't pick us off one at a time. Agreed?"

"Yeah," Rollins said.

"Let's watch our backs."

The three of them started walking toward the train cars, continuously looking around for signs of trouble. They fully expected to run into some. Once they got to the first car, they tried to open it, thinking someone may have been inside waiting for them, but it was locked. They continued on down their path, checking each car as they came across it. They also checked underneath. After scoping out about twenty cars with no results, they took a brief rest, still keeping their eyes peeled.

"Think maybe we got this wrong?" Rollins asked.

"Still another thirty cars or so to check," Cirella replied.

"Maybe he wasn't really setting us up. Maybe he just figured he could lose us here."

"Well, I guess we'll find out soon enough."

They started moving again, checking a few more cars. Doubt began to creep into their minds, wondering if maybe they were wasting their time. Maybe Falk wasn't trying to lead them anywhere. Maybe he just figured this was a good place to lose them. They soon found out that was not the case. A few more minutes went by, and Cirella tried to open another car, but it was locked. Hearing the men below, a man on top of the car jumped up and started firing. Cirella dove to the side, bullets just narrowly missing him and digging into the ground. Rollins and Brantly stood their ground, Brantly dropping to one knee, and both returning fire. They both hit the man who dropped his gun, the weapon falling down to the ground, and the man's body following soon after. Cirella got to his feet and went over to check on the man while Rollins and Brantly provided cover, looking around for the next shoe to drop. As Cirella checked the man, who was dead, he was a little disappointed that it wasn't Falk.

"It's not Danny," Cirella said.

"Who is it?" Rollins asked.

"Beats me."

"Guess that answers our question about whether we were set up."

"Sure does."

"Now the question is how many more?"

"I'd be surprised if it's only one," Cirella answered.

The men continued on, Cirella paying attention to the cars themselves, while Rollins checked underneath them, and Brantly kept his eyes glued to the roofs. They passed another car, then a shot rang out, ringing off the car that was next to them. Hearing that the shot came from behind them, they spun around, seeing the silhouette of a man about ten cars away. They returned fire, but the timing and distance seemed odd to Cirella, thinking that it might have been a diversion. Whoever it was couldn't have thought they'd kill them all from there. He looked at the car next to them and backed up, clearing the door. As Rollins and Brantly exchanged gunfire with the man, Cirella stood there, patiently waiting, thinking someone else was showing up soon. A minute later, he noticed the door to the car move, though it was only an inch or two. Someone was in there, waiting for just the right moment to shoot them all in the back. Cirella took a few steps back and pointed his gun at the car opening, waiting for the door to fully open and give himself a target to shoot at. After another twenty seconds, it finally happened.

The train car door finally slid open, a man appearing, armed with an automatic rifle. He pointed it at the direction of Rollins and Brantly. Cirella didn't let him get those shots off though. As soon as the man appeared, Cirella pumped a few rounds of lead into him, the man falling over backwards in the car. Rollins and Brantly jumped upon hearing the commotion behind them and turned around. They saw Cirella with his gun pointed at the car, then Brantly went over to inspect it. They shined a flashlight inside, then Brantly got in, checking the car for another shooter first. No one else was there except the now dead man. Brantly then jumped back out of the car.

"He's dead."

"Danny?" Rollins asked.

Brantly shook his head.

"How many more?"

They turned back to see if the silhouetted man was still visible, but he wasn't. He'd retreated to somewhere. He was too far away to tell if it was Falk or somebody else.

"Keep going?" Rollins asked, starting to think they should just get out of there before it got too hot.

"Yeah," Cirella answered, wanting to eliminate anyone who was there. He didn't want to have to deal with them later.

They kept on going, passing a couple more cars. Then suddenly, Rollins opened up on something underneath a car, firing multiple rounds at his target. Cirella and Brantly dropped to the ground and was about to join their friend, but Rollins quickly stopped. A cat sprinted out from underneath the car, running away from the men. Rollins let out a sigh, thinking he was getting jumpy. He looked at Cirella who just gave him a grin.

"Saw something move," Rollins said.

"Good thing cats got nine lives," Cirella replied. "Think he just used about six of them right there."

They moved on, with Cirella leading the way. They passed another car, then Rollins noticed a pair of legs waiting up ahead, seemingly lodged between two cars. He quickly picked up a stone and flung it at his boss, hitting Cirella in the back of the neck. Cirella rubbed his neck and turned around. Rollins put his index finger in the air to indicate it was just one man, then motioned between his index and middle fingers to let Cirella know the man was hiding between the cars. They could have tried to roll underneath the car and try to come up behind the man, but he most likely would have heard them rustling on the ground.

Cirella took a few more steps, until he was just about at the edge of the one car. He didn't even want to peek around the corner, fearing that his head would get shot off if he did. Knowing most people's first move was to look up when they were firing at a target, Cirella figured he could get the jump on him by being lower. Not even taking a few extra seconds to think about it, Cirella dove to the ground, firing between the cars as he did. The other man also fired, but Cirella was right in his assessment, as the man fired overtop of Cirella's falling body. Cirella's initial shots hit the man in the stomach, causing him to drop to the ground and hold his gut as blood started pouring out of him. He wasn't yet dead, but it wouldn't have taken too much longer.

Cirella picked himself up then walked over to the man who was on both his knees, holding his stomach. Rollins and Brantly also rushed over to him. Cirella kicked the man's gun away to make sure he didn't entertain any stupid thoughts. Before they were able to ask him any questions, they heard the squealing sounds of tires off in the distance. They snapped their heads in that direction, the tires sounding like it was coming from the area where they left their car. They had the suspicion that it was Falk getting away. As

Cirella was about to question the man, Rollins and Brantly stood guard, making sure there were no other surprises in store for them. Cirella squatted to get down to the injured man's level.

"Hey, let me ask you a couple questions."

"Just kill me and get it over with," the man said.

"I don't have any interest in doing that. Answer my questions and we'll get out of here. Then you can drive yourself to a hospital or call an ambulance, whatever you wanna do."

The man hunched over, feeling like his insides were on fire. "What do you want?"

"What were you here for? Who hired you?"

"Danny."

"How many of you are here?" Cirella asked.

"Four of us."

"Including Danny?"

"Yeah."

"What'd he want you guys to do? What'd he tell you?"

"He told us to spread out in different areas so we could surprise you. Said he was gonna lead you here."

Cirella looked at Rollins, their suspicions now confirmed that it was a setup, if it wasn't clear enough already.

"He wanted to kill us all here?" Cirella asked.

The man could only nod, the pain getting too intense to speak. Even nodding took a tremendous amount of energy. Cirella asked a couple more questions, but the man didn't seem to hear him. Looking like he was having trouble controlling his balance, Cirella put his hand on the man's shoulder to keep him upright. The man eventually closed his eyes though, and Cirella could tell that he was gone. The man's body slumped forward, and Cirella put both hands on him to prevent him from falling. Instead, Cirella gently placed his body on the ground. Even though the man tried to kill him, Cirella wasn't mad. Some people probably would have just let the man's body fall violently to the ground, angry about the events of the night, but Cirella wasn't one of them. He had no personal beef with the man and had enough respect for his opponents to not treat them with ill intent whether they were alive or not. Cirella stood back up and looked at the man, putting his gun back in its holster. Rollins and Brantly looked at him, wondering what their next steps were.

"What now?" Rollins asked.

"Let's get out of here," Cirella answered.

"What if there's still more out here?"

"He said there was only four including Danny."

"Maybe he was lying. Maybe that's part of the plan, that if any of them got captured, that's what they were supposed to say to throw us off-guard."

"No, I don't think so. I mean, if you guys wanna keep searching you can go ahead, but I'm out. I'm leaving. We're done here."

If Cirella was leaving, the other two certainly

weren't staying. Unlike their boss, though, they weren't putting their guns away until they were safely back in their vehicle. They cautiously walked back to their car, still keeping an eye out in case any other signs of trouble appeared. It was over though. Falk was the only one left of the group he hired to take out his former friends. The others were dead and he took off. Once Cirella and his team had returned to their vehicle, they just wanted to put the incident behind them, even though in the grand scheme of things, it wasn't over at all. Not until they dealt with their former partner.

"What about Danny?" Rollins asked.

"What about him?" Cirella replied.

"What are we gonna do with him?"

"Nothing really to talk about. He's a dead man. No talk, no discussion, no nothing. The next time I see him, doesn't matter where it is, in a park, at a shopping mall, in a restaurant, in the middle of the street, don't matter, he's dead. No questions asked. He's dead."

10

B y the time Carter got home from the meeting at the restaurant, the kids were already in bed. Stacy, though, was watching TV in the living room, waiting for her husband to get home. When Carter walked in, he was almost tip-toeing through the house, like he was afraid to let his wife know he was home. Maybe he was. He certainly wasn't looking forward to the talk he knew they were prob-ably going to have. He wasn't going to make up a story or lie to her. He had to be honest and tell her the truth, that he was rejoining the crew for one job.

Jack didn't tell her he was home, but she obviously heard him come in the door. He went straight to the kitchen and grabbed a drink, sitting down at the table. A few minutes later, his wife stood in the entranceway that led to the living room. She was leaning up against the wall with her arms folded. She didn't look like she was in a good mood. Jack briefly glanced up at her, then let his eyes return to the table. Seeing as how her husband wasn't talking, Stacy had a good idea what he'd agreed to. Nevertheless, she wanted to hear it out of his mouth. She walked over to the table and sat across from him.

"So, you gonna talk about it?"

"About what?" Jack asked.

"About what happened at the restaurant?"

"Just had dinner, talked about things."

"C'mon, Jack, let's not beat around the bush. I've had the kids all day and I'm tired. They obviously want you back on the team or they wouldn't have gone to all that trouble. Just tell me what you told them."

Jack cleared his throat and nervously wiped and scratched his face, worrying what her reaction would be. "I, uhh, told them that I would do one job."

Stacy shook her head as she looked away. "I knew it. I knew they'd rope you in."

"It's only one job, Stacy, OK? Just one. It's not a big deal. I'm not rejoining the group permanently, I'm not abandoning you guys, everything's gonna be fine after the one job."

"One, huh?"

"Yes, one. That's it. I do one job and then I'm out."

"Yeah, we'll see."

Stacy doubted whether Cirella would let him go that easily once he got his hooks back into him. Especially if their job went off without a hitch. In that case, Cirella was going to want to keep things going.

"This could really change things for us."

"Oh, I'm well aware," she said.

Jack rolled his eyes and sighed. Now he was the one frustrated. "All you do is look at the negative side of things and the bad things that can happen."

"Yeah, and you should be looking at them too."

"This job could give us over a hundred thousand dollars. That would look pretty nice in our bank account, wouldn't it?"

"All you're looking at is the money. That's it."

"And all you're looking at is what could go wrong."

"And what exactly is the job that you're doing?" Stacy asked. "Hope you're not robbing some old lady of her life's savings."

"It's an armored car. I wouldn't partake in something against an innocent person."

Stacy huffed, then look at the ceiling, completely vexed. She put her hands on her face, then ran them up her head and through her hair, holding them on the back of her neck for a minute as she tried to process everything.

"An armored car. Couldn't have found something even harder?" Stacy sarcastically asked.

Jack's hand rose from the table to stop her from going on. "It's a good plan. They already went over everything with me. As long as everyone does their job, there should be no complications."

"Jack, there's always complications."

"Not with this. They've got everything laid out perfectly. There's nothing to worry about."

"And where's the money coming from? A bank?"

Jack shrugged,. "I don't really know. They didn't say. It doesn't really matter, does it? Wherever it's coming from has insurance for that sort of thing. They won't be out anything. They'll get their money back."

"Except the insurance company will be out the money."

"Please, insurance companies have more money than they know what to do with. They're as much a bunch of crooks as anyone else, always raising rates, denying claims, screwing the little and poor people."

"That's not really the point," Stacy said.

"It's exactly the point. No matter what I say or do you're gonna find fault with it."

"That's not true. I just don't want you to wind up in a prison cell."

"And I won't. I promise."

"I guess we know what that's worth, don't we?"

"What's that supposed to mean?" Jack asked.

"You promised me once before you were done with all this. Guess your word's not good enough, is it?"

"Don't be like that."

"And when is this job supposed to take place?"

"Next week."

Stacy's jaw tightened, looking madder than ever. "I

want you to call Dom back right now and tell him you changed your mind."

"What?"

"I want you to call him back and tell him you're not gonna do it."

"I can't do that."

"Why not?"

"Because I already told him I would."

"So change your mind."

"I can't do that. I've already seen the plans, I know the job, I can't pull out now."

"I can't believe you've done this to us."

"Done what? Trying to make a better life for us?"

"No, put us in a situation that we might lose you."

Jack sat up straighter and threw his hands in the air, letting them slam down on the table. He was frustrated with her attitude and didn't know what else to say. His decision was made and he didn't want to argue about it with her anymore. Stacy was also frustrated and didn't want to argue about it either. She realized his mind was made up, and nothing she was going to say would change that.

"Maybe I should just take the kids to my parents for a week or two."

"Why?" Jack asked.

"Because I don't know if I want them here with you while you're doing this."

"Stacy, don't be like that."

She got up and began to walk out of the room. "I don't know if I wanna be here with you either."

Jack watched his wife leave, then put his head in his hands, thinking this couldn't have turned out any worse. The only thing he could hope for is that she changed her mind after a good night's sleep. But knowing his wife, he wouldn't count on it.

AFTER LEAVING THE TRAIN YARD, Cirella and company immediately went to Falk's apartment, hoping they could catch him by surprise somehow. They were sitting in a parking spot, further down in the lot, though they could still see Falk's door from where they were. But they didn't want to be right in front of the apartment so Falk could look out the window and see them sitting there.

"You really think he's in there?" Rollins asked.

"I dunno," Cirella answered. "Doesn't hurt to sit here and wait though."

"He's not coming back here. His car's not here. There's no way he's dumb enough to pull that stunt then come back here. He knows we'd show up looking for him."

"People do dumb things all the time. Maybe he didn't figure on us escaping from that place. Maybe he still needs to pack up. Maybe a lot of things. We got nothing else to check on right now, so it doesn't hurt to make sure."

"I get all that. I'm just saying I don't think he's coming."

"We'll see."

They sat there for over two hours without the slightest movement around the apartment. They didn't see Falk's car drive by, or a door open, or a curtain move, nothing. Though Cirella knew it was probably a longshot, he was now swinging around to Rollins' point. Falk wasn't showing up.

"What do you say we take a look inside?" Brantly asked.

"You took the words right out of my mouth," Cirella replied.

"What for?" Rollins asked.

"Maybe he left behind a clue to where he's at or where he's going. Doesn't hurt to check, right?"

"I guess."

The three men got out of their car and walked over to Falk's apartment. The door was locked, but Rollins had it open in less than a minute. They flicked on a light and started looking around. Cirella wanted to make sure they had no more surprises in store for them.

"Isaac, you keep an eye on the street. I wanna make sure this isn't another setup or something, and he starts blasting us through the windows."

"Sure thing," Brantly said, going over to the window.

Cirella started searching through the living room while Rollins went into the kitchen. They weren't turning up much. The place was pretty messy, with mostly trash and food wrappers on the floor, but they didn't find anything that appeared to give them a clue as to where Falk was.

"Doesn't look like he's been here for a few days," Rollins said.

"How you know?" Cirella asked.

"Lack of food. Fridge is bare. Cabinets are empty."

"Maybe he's been eating out a lot."

They finished searching their respective rooms and started toward the bedroom.

"Anything out there?" Cirella asked.

"No, looking pretty clear," Brantly answered.

"Let's hope it stays that way," Rollins said.

Cirella and Rollins then went into the bedroom, tearing it apart, looking under the mattress, inside the closet, through the dresser drawers, end tables, everything that could have hid anything, they checked it. There was nothing there.

"Clothes are gone," Rollins said. "Face it, he's a ghost."

"Yeah," Cirella said with a sigh.

Finished with the bedroom, they checked the bathroom, not that they expected to find anything there.

And they were right. Falk didn't leave anything behind. Not even a toothbrush.

"What now?" Rollins asked.

"Now we take it on the road," Cirella said.

The two went back into the living room and met up with Brantly again.

"Maybe we should mention it to Mark," Rollins said. "Maybe he can figure something out."

"It's a loose end that we don't need right now," Cirella said.

"At least he doesn't know anything about the armored car. If he did, that'd put everything in jeopardy. As it stands right now, he's just a pain in our ass. Nothing more."

"I don't like having this hang over our heads."

"Just gotta keep our eyes open."

"He knows where we all live. We have to be careful."

"You think he's gonna keep trying to pick us off?" Brantly asked.

"I think if he tried once, he'll try again," Cirella said. "And at our homes, we're more vulnerable. We're by ourselves. If he gets a few more guys together, who knows what he'll do?"

"Well, he won't try anything tonight," Rollins said.

"You sure about that? You know where he is right now?"

Rollins was silent, just looking at his two partners. Cirella was right. He didn't like not knowing where

Falk was at the moment, not knowing what he was planning.

"What do we do?" Brantly asked.

"I think it's best if we stick together a few days," Cirella replied.

"Probably for the best," Rollins said.

"I can't wait 'till this is all over," Brantly said.

"I can't wait 'till that jerk is in the ground," Cirella added. "As soon as possible."

11

F alk was led into the interview room where he waited for the detectives to come in and talk to him. He'd been in jail all night, ever since fleeing the train yard. Going down the highway at over ninety miles per hour, he was pulled over for speeding. Then the officers suspected him of being under the influence and got him out of the car. He failed the breathalyzer test, the officers found narcotics in the car, as well as several weapons. Knowing he was probably going to be put away for a long time, Falk asked to speak with someone about cutting a deal.

The door opened and two detectives stepped inside. One was Lieutenant Downing, a twenty-year veteran. He was about six feet tall, more on the thin side, but had a grizzled face that suggested he'd been through the wringer. He was considered a bit of a hard-nose, unsympathetic at times in his pursuit of suspects. All that mattered to him was getting the job done in whatever way was necessary. He wasn't against bending the rules to suit what he needed as long as it didn't seriously cross the line. But at times he'd hop over that line.

The other man was Detective Gruber, who'd been a detective for ten years. Downing's unit was usually the first one called for major cases. Murders, robberies, high-profile cases, they were considered the best. They were relentless in their pursuit of suspects. Some in the department joked that the team never stopped working, never left the office, and didn't have a life outside of the department. There was some level of truth in that. Downing was divorced and without children, so he put everything into his work. It wasn't uncommon for him to work fifteen-hour days. He had four other men in his unit, and only one was married. And that detective still worked twelve-hour days. They were just devoted to their work and took a lot of pride in what they did. They didn't even mind working off the clock if that's what was necessary. And they did it often.

Downing and Gruber sat across from Falk. Downing put down a file folder with Falk's history and background inside. Gruber set down a pad of paper and a pen so he could write notes. Falk was considered a dangerous man, and the police were well acquainted with his name already, as he was rumored to have been involved in several robberies that they were already looking into.

"Before we get started, my name is Lieutenant Downing, and this is Detective Gruber. I hear you requested us."

"If you're the top guys. If you're the guys to talk to about making a deal," Falk replied.

"Well, that would depend on what you have to say."

"I've been involved in some things. Can give you names, dates, places, things like that."

Downing wasn't yet impressed. He'd heard the claims before from various criminals, and sometimes the information wasn't worth much. "In return for what?"

"I don't wanna go to jail."

"Too late for that. You're going. You've been caught and booked. Nothing changes that."

"You can put a word in for a reduction though. No more than one year, max."

Downing quickly glanced at Gruber. "That would entirely depend on the information. Right now, you're a convicted felon carrying a gun, narcotics, and with your record, you're probably looking at three to five."

"Like I said... one... max."

"If that's what you're looking for, you better open up and tell me where the Holy Grail is."

"Before I start talking, I need assurances," Falk said.

"If what you say has value, I'll put a word in. But it better be damn good. If you tell me about a bunch of high school kids bullying a classmate and stealing his lunch money, you're gonna be looking at my ass walking out of here."

Falk grinned, knowing he could say enough interesting things that would knock the detective's socks off. "Yeah, I got some stuff for you."

"Well, then let's stop horse-puckering around and get to it. I got things to do, people to lock up."

"You know Dominic Cirella?"

Downing immediately glanced over at his partner, their ears instantly pricking up. They'd heard the name enough times to garner their interest. "Yeah, I know him."

"Well, I was part of his crew."

"Was?"

Falk shrugged, like it wasn't a big deal, like he didn't just try to have his former crew killed in a fit of rage. He tried to downplay it so it didn't seem like he was just going after them for revenge. "We had a bit of a falling out. A slight disagreement so we decided to part ways."

"So, what can you tell me about him? Who else is in his crew?"

"Isaac Brantly. Noah Rollins."

"That it?"

"Yeah."

"What about you?" Downing asked. "Nobody replaced you? How long ago did you leave?"

"Uhh, few weeks ago."

"You haven't really told us anything new here. We already know about Cirella and his crew. They're always under suspicion for pulling jobs."

"Yeah, but you never had anything concrete against them before or else they'd be in jail. At least until now."

"So name a job they've been involved in recently."

"You know about that Montgomery job in the past week?" Falk said. "The guy who got killed in his house and had his diamonds and jewelry stolen?"

"Yeah, what of it?"

"That was them."

"Cirella and his crew pulled that off?"

Downing looked over at Gruber, who was writing everything down. "You sure about that?"

"Oh yeah."

"How do you know?"

"I was supposed to be in on it."

"You were?" Downing asked. "So you're telling me you weren't there?"

Falk shook his head. "No way, man."

"Why not?"

"I told you. Me and Cirella had a difference of opinion so we decided to go our separate ways."

"And what difference of opinion would that be?"

"Killing, for one. He was all about it. Said we should just take down whoever gets in our way. I didn't want no part of that, man. I just wanted to do the job and get out. Nobody needed to get hurt."

"And Cirella thought differently?"

"Yeah. Like I said, he's been getting more and more violent, not caring about hurting anyone who gets in his way. That's why I wanted out."

"And he just let you out? Just like that? Knowing you knew their plans, their history, everything about them... and they just let you leave?" Downing asked, sounding extremely skeptical.

"They didn't have any concerns about you blowing the whistle on them or anything?" Gruber added, finally getting in a question.

Falk shrugged again. "Guess they trusted me. We left on good terms and all."

Downing smirked and looked at his partner. He knew that most times when a guy was informing on a former partner, it usually wasn't because they were on good terms. Especially a guy like Cirella, who had a high-profile name. When a guy was blowing the whistle like this, it was usually because they got burned somehow, or felt slighted in some way. Downing was getting the feeling this was one of those times. Falk had all the makings of a guy who was untrustworthy. The detectives had seen his kind before. Guys who were on good terms with their partners kept their mouths shut even if they were looking at a long prison term. Stretches that were a lot longer than the one that Falk was looking at. He was only looking at less than five years. Some guys could do that standing on their head. No, the only reason Falk was informing now was because he felt slighted somehow. Maybe he got kicked out and this was revenge. Downing didn't know and was sure he wouldn't get the answer, at least not a truthful answer, but in the end it didn't really matter why. All that mattered was that the information was correct.

"What were you doing last night?" Downing asked.

"Last night?"

"Yeah. You were caught with a gun that you shouldn't have, that you're not supposed to have. Not only that, there were bullets missing, and according to the arresting officers, it smelled like it was recently fired."

"Just target practice."

"Where?"

"Train yard."

Downing and Gruber looked at each other again. "Oh, you mean the train yard that we discovered three dead bodies in? That train yard?"

Falk put his hand over his head, not even thinking about the bodies. "Listen, that wasn't me."

"Oh, it wasn't? Who was it then?"

"It was Cirella, man. His crew. They were all there."

"Why?"

"They were gunning for me. I had to protect myself."

"They were gunning for you?" Downing asked, raising his voice. "You just told us you guys had no problems. You said you left the crew without any issues. Now they're trying to kill you?"

"What is this, an inquisition? I'm giving you this crew on a silver platter and you're acting like you don't want it."

"What I want is the truth. And I'm not sure I'm getting it from you, because my bullshit meter is ringing off the charts right now."

Falk shrugged. "Hey, you do whatever you want, man. You don't wanna believe me that's your problem. I'm telling you the truth."

"How do I know you didn't whack those guys at the train yard? How do I know you're not just making up some story, trying to put the blame on some poor slob so you can be in the clear?"

Falk was quiet for a few seconds, alternating between staring at the two detectives sitting in front of him. "You got all this high-tech at your disposal now, right? Check my gun. Ballistics will tell you I didn't shoot those guys. Those bullets didn't come from my gun."

"Who were you shooting at?" Gruber asked.

"Already told you. Cirella and his crew."

"And who were these other guys?"

"Who?" Falk asked.

"The dead guys. Who are they? Not part of Cirella's crew, are they?"

"No, just some guys I knew."

"What were you doing there?" Downing asked.

"Just taking a midnight stroll with your friends? Just happened to meet up with your former crew?

"Listen, I got word that they might have been looking for me. So I wanted to protect myself."

"Most guys looking to protect themselves don't take a bunch of other thugs to a deserted train yard late at night, armed to the teeth, do they?"

Falk was quiet again, trying to think up a new story that he thought the detectives would buy. "OK, I'll give it to you straight."

"Oh great, this should be good!" Downing said, chuckling to himself.

"We didn't end on such good terms. I wasn't on board with the Montgomery job, like I told you already. Cirella didn't like me walking around, knowing about what happened, thinking I might be a loose end."

"Looks like he might have been right there, huh?"

"Anyway, I heard he wanted to take me out that way he didn't have to worry about me anymore. So I got some guys together, let Cirella and his crew know I was gonna be there, and figured I'd be proactive and take them out first. Just didn't turn out like I planned."

Downing laughed. "Boy, I'd say it didn't. Your friends are dead, you're locked up in here, and Cirella and his crew are walking the streets free and easy. Couldn't get a worse result than that, could you?"

"Yeah, you could be dead too," Gruber said.

Falk smirked, knowing he seemed to have bungled

things. All he could do now was try to worm his way out of it.

"So you're telling me Cirella pulled that Montgomery job, without you, and that he killed Montgomery?" Downing asked.

"That's right," Falk replied.

"Why? Why would he do that?"

Falk shrugged. "Search me. He's kind of a loose cannon."

"That runs counter to everything we've ever heard about the man. Only thing I've ever heard is that he's cautious, low-key, is a meticulous planner, doesn't fly by the seat of his pants, doesn't try to draw attention to himself, and here you are telling me he goes around killing people at the drop of a hat."

"He's got a top-of-the-line crew," Gruber said. "He doesn't need to kill an unarmed man to take his jewels."

"So what? You think I'm making it up?" Falk asked.

"Maybe fabricating some of it?" Downing said.

"It's just like I told you."

"What kind of evidence do you have to corroborate that?"

"Evidence?"

"Yeah, you know, like proof. You got something?"

"Like what?"

"I dunno," Downing said. "Like anything."

"Isn't my word good enough?"

Downing snickered, putting his hand over his eyes

for a moment, already feeling like he put in a twenty-hour day. "As much as I believe that you're an upstanding citizen who's just trying to help us, I need more than just your word to go into a courtroom. I need proof. Evidence that Cirella was there."

"I'm telling you how it was."

"Unfortunately, the court tends to frown upon he said, she said types of situations. They don't know who to believe, and frankly, neither do I. I need to either catch them in the act of doing something, them getting rid of the merchandise, matching up the car that they used to a tire track, something like that. That's what I need. Evidence."

Falk sat up a little straighter, knowing he had to give them more. "I can give you everything you need. All their addresses, the cars they drive, even their storage unit."

"Storage unit?"

"They got a storage unit. They park the car they use in there, that way if it's spotted on a job, they're not driving around the street with it, or taking the risk of getting pulled over."

Downing nodded, feeling like he was finally getting something useful. "Nice. That's what we can use to build a case."

Gruber turned his pad around, slapped the pen down on it, then slid it across the table to Falk.

"Write down everything you know," Gruber said. "Their home addresses, cars they have, license plates, anybody else they know and do business with, and the address and unit number of that storage facility."

Falk grabbed the pen and immediately started writing everything he knew. It took a few minutes for him to write it all down, making sure he didn't put down anything else that would further incriminate him somehow. When he was done, he put the pen back down on the pad and slid it over to the detective. Gruber moved the pad halfway between him and Downing that way they both could look it over at the same time.

"Who's this Mark fellow?" Downing asked.

"Kind of a bigshot," Falk answered. "He kind of facilitates things."

"He's the head guy?"

"No, not really. I mean, when he gets wind of something, he passes it along to a certain crew that he thinks is good for the job, then he takes a cut out of the haul."

"He's an information guy?"

"Yeah, pretty much."

"How many crews does he use?"

"I dunno, beats me. Half a dozen, ten, twelve, I really don't know."

"What's his last name?" Downing asked.

"Couldn't tell you. Never heard it."

"How often did you meet with him?"

"Not much. Only two or three times when it was

necessary. He usually only meets with the crew leaders. That way he cuts down his risk."

"Smart."

"Yeah."

"So, where's he live?" Gruber asked.

"Again, couldn't tell you. Never been there, never heard it mentioned."

"And you never asked?"

"Listen, when you're running with these crews, you only ask what pertains to you," Falk replied. "Everything else is on a need to know basis. And if you need to ask, you probably don't need to know. Whoever's in charge of the crew tells you what he thinks is necessary. Everything else is just fat."

"So you don't really know anything about this Mark guy?" Downing asked.

"Not really."

"He an ex-con, on the run, businessman, the mayor?"

"Just know he's well-respected. Don't know anything about him other than that."

"You think you could describe him if we hooked you up with a sketch artist?"

Falk nodded. "Yeah, I can pin him down for you, no sweat."

"What about Cirella? He planning anything right now? Got a job lined up?"

"That I don't know. Wouldn't surprise me if he did.

He's always on the lookout for something. But I couldn't say for sure."

Downing tapped Gruber on the forearm, indicating that they were done for the time being. Gruber grabbed his pad and put his pen in his pocket.

"OK, so what we're gonna do is check out some of this information," Downing said. "You're gonna go back to your holding cell for now. We'll set something up with a sketch artist."

"What about our deal?" Falk asked.

"If this information checks out, we'll have more to talk about."

"All right. It will."

Downing and Gruber left the interview room and walked back to their office. They sat down at their desks and discussed what they just heard.

"What do you think?" Gruber asked. "You think he's telling the truth?"

"I think it's one of those half-and-half type of deals. Some of it's probably true, some of it's probably a lie, and some of it is true enough to fit the story he wants to tell."

"You think they're good for that Montgomery job?"

Downing grimaced, not so sure. "I dunno. There's something weird about that. The crew is good enough to get in there, subdue a guard without killing him, get out of the house before the police get there from the alarm, you really think they're gonna panic and kill an unarmed man? One who probably doesn't pose any threat to them? Doesn't make sense to me."

"If they were planning on killing Montgomery, why not just kill the guard to begin with?"

"Exactly," Downing said. "The whole thing doesn't make sense. And it doesn't fit what we've heard about Cirella's crew. There's more to that story than he's telling."

"Still, he gave us names and addresses."

"And we'll look into it for sure. Even if we can't pin Cirella down for the Montgomery job, maybe we can get some kind of evidence from other jobs from that storage unit."

"Or we can stake out their homes, follow them, maybe catch them in the act."

"I agree."

"What do you wanna do first?"

"First thing we gotta do is get a warrant to check out that storage unit," Downing said. "I don't wanna make any contact with that crew, interview, follow, nothing, until we've looked inside that unit. Because if they know we're coming before we check that place out, it'll be a ghost town by the time we get to it. And I don't want them to see us coming."

12

Cirella, Rollins, and Brantly had just finished eating breakfast in Cirella's apartment, with him making eggs and toast for everyone since Rollins and Brantly slept on his couches for the night. After clearing the dishes and putting them in the sink, they sat back down at the table to discuss their plans for the day. Falk was still front and center on their minds. They'd only gotten a couple of minutes into their conversation when Cirella's phone started ringing. He wasn't expecting a call, but when he saw it was Mark, he figured it was more information about the armored car job.

"Hey, got some news for you."

"What's up?" Cirella asked.

"Danny's in the tank."

"What?"

"Cops picked him up last night."

"We had a run-in with him last night," Cirella said. "He grabbed some boys and tried to ambush us in a train yard."

Knowing they were talking about Falk, Rollins and Brantly turned toward Cirella to try to listen in to the conversation and pick up whatever bits and pieces they could.

"Yeah, I heard about that," Mark said. "They must've picked him up right after that."

"What'd they grab him for?"

"Uhh, bunch of things, I think. Speeding, driving under the influence, firearm possession, drug paraphernalia... I think that was it. That's enough to put him away for a few years."

"At least. That'll make us sleep a little easier for now."

"I don't know about that," Mark said.

"Why not?"

"I heard he's been doing some singing."

"He's flipping?"

"I don't have to give you two guesses what he's talking about."

"Us."

"You got it. My contact on the inside said he's pinning the Montgomery murder on you specifically, and he's giving up your addresses, cars, everything."

Cirella knew what that meant. His mind immediately turned to their storage unit, knowing the police would be there soon to search through it.

"How much time do we have?"

"They're waiting on a judge's signature now," Mark replied. "I would guess you got an hour or two. Three at the most depending on whatever else he's got on his desk."

Cirella took the phone away from his mouth to address his friends. "Go clean out the unit now. We got an hour."

Rollins and Brantly rushed out of the apartment. They'd always had a plan in place for a moment like this. They knew eventually there would come a time when something like this happened. It just came sooner than they'd expected. Cirella pressed the phone back to his ear to continue his conversation.

"This is gonna complicate things," Mark said.

"I know it."

"The job's still gonna be a go, but you're gonna have to navigate the cops now, because it's a sure thing they'll be looking at you."

Cirella sighed, knowing how complicated things were getting now. "I should've killed Danny when I had the chance."

"Don't beat yourself up over it. You gave him a chance. He blew it."

"Yeah, but now we're gonna have the heat coming down on us from all directions. What do you know about who's taking the case?"

"It's a Lieutenant Downing," Mark said, reading the

information off a piece of paper. "He's a bit of a hard-nose. Dedicated guy. Leads a unit."

"So we're gonna have to watch our p's and q's."

"Oh yeah. Definitely. This guy isn't some slob who just wants to put his time in and go home. He's one of those guys who wants to make a difference, get every bad guy off the street, one of those types. He keeps coming 'till he gets who he's after."

"You know what his play is after he searches the storage unit?" Cirella asked.

"Don't know for sure yet. You can bet your bottom dollar that he's gonna tail you guys."

"We'll keep an eye out."

"If the heat gets too hot and you need to bail on the job..."

"No, we'll pull the job off, heat or not."

Cirella didn't care who was looking at him or coming after him. He wasn't about to walk away from a job that would net him over a hundred thousand dollars. Maybe if it was a smaller score, it'd be an easier decision, but not with so much money at stake. He went over to the window and looked out the blinds to see if he could spot a car staking out his place. There was nobody there. He could usually tell if there was something not right.

"You gotta be careful."

"We'll be fine," Cirella said. "If we gotta hide out in some dump for a week, then that's what we'll do."

"You might not get the chance."

"If they find us before we're able to do that, then we'll take an alternate course. We'll be OK though. Won't be the first time the heat's been on me."

"I know. I just wanna make sure it's not the last."

They talked a few different scenarios for another ten minutes or so before getting off the phone. Cirella jetted out of his apartment to meet his friends at the storage facility. By the time he got there, Rollins and Brantly had everything well under control. Thankfully the police weren't there yet. They didn't usually keep much on the floors anyway, but any bags or guns they had just lying around, they threw in the SUV. Within ten minutes, they were ready to go. Brantly got into the SUV and drove it off while the others got back into their cars and followed it. They had a backup unit ready, about twenty minutes away, that was already paid for. They also had a third unit, clear across on the other side of the city, just in case they were on a job on that side and things got too hot, they could ditch it easily. It was all part of the planning to make sure they had all their bases covered. Cirella had several backup units that he never told Falk about, mostly because he didn't trust him as much as the others. And he told the rest of the crew to never mention the other units to Falk unless they absolutely needed to use them. Once the car was secured again in the new unit, Rollins wanted to know the plan from there.

"What are we gonna do now?"

"You guys should probably hit your apartments,

pack up real quick, take whatever you need for the next week or so," Cirella said.

"Where do we go from there?"

"Go back to my place. We'll figure it out from there."

"You coming?"

"I'll be there. I wanna go back to the unit and see if the cops show up."

"Why you wanna do that?"

"Curious to see if they actually come," Cirella answered.

"And if they do? What's that gonna accomplish?"

"I wanna know for sure whether Danny's singing or not. If they show up, we know he is."

"You're taking chances."

"Nah. What are they gonna do? Arrest me for sitting there?"

"Danny could've told them a lot of stuff," Rollins said, fearful he might have said too much.

"There's nothing he could've told them that could incriminate us without incriminating himself."

"Unless he strikes a deal."

"Let him strike one. Let him talk. It'll be his word against ours. As far as I'm concerned, he doesn't have a good enough track record to be believed. And there's still a thing called due process in this country. If they wanna convict, they'll need proof, not hearsay. And they don't have it."

"All right, hope you know what you're doing."

"It'll be fine," Cirella said. "You guys get going."

Cirella drove back to the original storage unit and waited in his car parked on the street just outside of the entrance. He didn't have long to wait. About ten minutes later, he noticed several unmarked police cars drive into the facility, along with two patrol cars. There was no doubt what they were there for. Mark's information was good, not that Cirella really had any doubts that it was, but it was good to see it confirmed.

Cirella kept his eyes on the unit, seeing all the police cars pull up in front of it. A man walked up to the door with some bolt cutters and sliced off the padlock. As one of the officers pulled the door open, Downing and his team started approaching the unit. Once the door was fully open, Downing, Gruber, and several other detectives stood there, staring into an empty unit.

"Sons of bitches," Downing said with a sigh.

"They knew we were coming," Gruber replied.

Downing walked into the unit and started looking around. "There's no doubt about that. No doubt at all."

"How? How could they know?"

"They must have some pretty good sources somewhere along the line."

"Maybe that Mark guy Falk was talking about."

"Yeah, could be."

They walked around the unit, but there was nothing to look at. They got out their flashlights and started inspecting the floor and around the base of the walls, hoping to find something, anything, a piece of thread, a cloth, something other than dust that would indicate the unit had been recently used. After a few minutes, they came up just as empty as the unit itself. The detectives then walked back outside.

"Well, that's a kick in the nuts," Gruber said. "What now?"

"I still want everything fingerprinted in there," Downing answered. "At least we can prove that they were actually here. Maybe pick up a tire tread or something."

As the team started fingerprinting both inside and outside the unit, Downing and Gruber stood outside of it, discussing what to do next.

"You think Falk was telling the truth about this?" Gruber asked.

"Never know with these guys. Some of them will say just about anything to get out of the trouble they're in."

While they were waiting for the fingerprinting and forensics team to get through with the unit, Downing started pacing around. He often did that when he was trying to think. After a minute or so, an eerie feeling came over him that they were being watched. He stopped what he was doing and started turning around, looking in all directions. He finally turned around fully and looked at the street, observing a car sitting by the entrance, with a male occupant just staring back at him.

"Cirella," Downing said, barely above a whisper.

"What was that?" Gruber asked.

"Cirella," Downing said, this time much louder, in his usual forceful sounding voice.

"Where?"

"Right there." Downing flicked his wrist into the air to point at the vehicle, then let out a laugh, amused by the situation. "He's sitting right there looking at us."

Gruber stood beside his boss and looked out at the street, also seeing the car. "What's he doing?"

Downing laughed again. "He's toying with us. He's taunting us."

"Why would he want to do that?"

"He wants us to know that he knows."

"A little cocky."

Downing shook his head, getting a completely different point of view. "No, this guy's good. He's so confident that he doesn't care." Then another thought came to him. "We're not going to find anything in there."

"Why not?"

"Look at this guy. He's just sitting there like he doesn't have a care in the world. And you know why that is?"

"Why?"

"Because he doesn't," Downing said. "He's got nothing to worry about. He knows there's nothing in there to find. Nothing that's gonna come back to him. Nothing that's gonna link him to that unit. They've probably already wiped it clean. They got word that we were coming and wiped it. These guys are good."

"Maybe we should have a word."

Downing didn't respond and seemed indifferent to the suggestion. Gruber didn't wait for confirmation to go and started walking towards Cirella's car. He got about halfway there, then Cirella put the car in drive. The detectives watched Cirella's car as it drove away.

"C'mon," Downing said.

"What?"

Downing started walking back to his car. "We gotta go."

"Where we going?" Gruber asked, walking quickly to catch up.

"We need to talk to these guys."

"What about the storage unit?"

Downing waved his hand at it, knowing it would come up empty. "That's a dead end, don't even worry about it. Those guys got it under control."

As the two detectives got back in their blue unmarked car, Gruber still wasn't sure what they were doing. "Where are we going?"

"You got Cirella's address down there?"

Gruber opened a file folder. "Yeah."

"Give it to me. That's where we're going."

Gruber told him the address, but wasn't sure it would do much good. "He probably won't be there. If they knew we were hitting this place, then I'm sure they've bolted."

"Maybe. We'll see. You got the other guys at Rollins and Brantly' places?"

"Yeah, should be there."

"Call them up and see if they got anything."

Gruber called the other detectives who were on stakeout duties at the addresses of both Rollins and Brantly.

"Not there," Gruber reported.

"Damn."

"I told you, they're gone. They're in the wind. They're not going back there."

"We'll swing by Cirella's address just in case and sit on it for a while."

"Then what?"

"Then we got work to do."

13

All the detective teams were in their respective spots for about two hours. There was no sign of any of their targets. Downing was close to calling it a day, figuring their time would be better spent elsewhere. Then his eyes were drawn to a car pulling in the parking lot of Cirella's apartment complex. It was a car he recognized.

"I don't believe it," Downing said.

"What?" Gruber asked.

"It's him."

"Who?"

"Cirella. He's pulling in now."

"Are you kidding?"

The two detectives watched as the car drove past them, each of them getting a clear look at Cirella in the driver's seat. They waited until Cirella parked and got out of his car before doing anything.

"You wanna go?" Gruber asked.

"Let's give him a few minutes to get situated."

Cirella walked on the grass and took a glance over at the detective's car, noticing that it was the same men he saw at the storage unit.

"He made us," Downing said.

"And he doesn't seem to care," Gruber replied.

"Nope. Not this guy. He's as cool as a cucumber."

"We just gonna wait here?"

"Ehh, for a bit. We'll see about the others. Maybe they're getting home about now too."

Gruber then noticed two other cars pulling in. He kept an eye on them as they parked. "I wouldn't count on it."

"Huh? Why not?"

Gruber pointed to the two men getting out of their cars. "'Cause they're right there."

Downing snapped his head to the side, seeing the two men go to the front of the building. "Are you kidding me? Are you kidding me?"

"They know we're watching."

A smile came over Downing's face, appearing to have an appreciation for the group they were watching. "These guys are brazen. I like it. They don't care who's watching them, they're just gonna go on about their business."

"You want me to call the other guys off or bring them here?"

"Tell them to take off for a bit. We'll handle this here."

"We're not gonna be able to follow all of them," Gruber said.

"We don't need to follow all of them. They're a team, right?"

"Yeah."

"So they're not doing anything without all of them together," Downing said. "We only need to follow one of them. We'll tail Cirella. He's the leader. They're not doing anything without him. He's the one calling the shots."

After ten minutes ticked by, Downing was getting antsy, not wanting to sit there anymore. He wanted to provoke some kind of response from Cirella, and he couldn't do that by sitting around. He wanted to talk face to face. The detectives got out of the car and started walking for the front door. They were being watched the whole time by Cirella, though, who was looking at them through the blinds of his window.

"I don't understand what we're doing, Dom," Rollins said. "The cops are onto us, why are we just sitting here like ducks on a pond, waiting for them to pick us off?"

Cirella turned to him and grinned. "Who's picking off who?"

"What are you talking about?"

"We got a job coming up next week, right?"

"Yeah."

"We know the heat's on us, right?"

"Again, yeah."

"So, what's the better option?" Cirella asked. "Going around, doing our thing, not knowing where these guys are? Or letting them think they've got us, letting them follow us around for a few days, knowing where they're at, then when the time is right, pow, we lose them, and do our thing, knowing they can't be there to screw it up?"

Rollins and Brantly looked at each other, knowing it made sense, but not sure they could pull it off.

Brantly shook his head. "I can't believe Danny did this to us."

"I can," Cirella replied. "He's a hothead and a weasel. We were right to let him go. We can't worry about that now. Now we just have to move forward."

With the detectives no longer visible now that they were inside the building, Cirella finally tore himself away from the window. He just stood there, staring at the door, waiting for the knock. The others wondered what he was doing. They each looked at the door, wondering what the problem was.

"What is it?" Rollins asked.

"We're about to get a visit."

Rollins got worried, his eyes opening wide and looking at the window, knowing he was referring to the detectives outside. "They're coming up?"

"Looks that way," Cirella replied, not an ounce of worry inside him.

"Should we scatter?"

"No, we're good. I told you they'd be here watching when I told you to meet me here."

"Yeah, but I didn't know that meant we were gonna be interviewed."

"I'll do the talking."

A few minutes later there was finally a knock on the door. Rollins and Brantly moved next to each other on the couch, keeping the door in full view. Cirella went over to the door and opened it, seeing the two detectives standing there.

"Dominic Cirella?" Downing asked.

"That's right."

"I'm Lieutenant..."

Cirella cut him off right away to let him know that he wasn't as in command as he thought he was. "Lieutenant Downing," Cirella said with a smile, like he was revealing a big secret that nobody was supposed to know. He then looked to the man's partner. "And you're... Gruber, is that right?"

The two detectives looked at each other, surprised that he knew their names. For Downing though, somehow, it wasn't a surprise at all. Cirella wasn't some run-of-the-mill criminal. He was extremely good. Maybe the best. He wasn't going to be tripped up by something trivial. If Downing was going to catch him, he was going to have to work at it. Maybe harder than he had ever worked on any case before.

Cirella put his arm out to welcome the two men. "Come on in."

"Just to be clear, we don't have a warrant or anything," Downing said. "We just came here to talk."

"That's all right. You don't need a warrant. If you want to search the place, you can. You have my permission."

"You guys don't have any guns in here, right?" Gruber asked.

"I'm sure you guys know we spent time in the cooler. As convicted felons. It would be illegal for us to own firearms or have them in our possession. But like I said, if you wanna search the place, go right ahead."

"No, that won't be necessary," Downing said. "I think we all know we wouldn't find anything in here."

"Why is that?"

"Because we both know you're too smart for that, don't we?"

Cirella made a face that he agreed and nodded. "Would you guys like to sit down?"

"No thanks," Downing answered. "We'll stand." He then looked at the two men sitting innocently on the couch, twiddling their thumbs. "Isaac Brantly and Noah Rollins, I presume?"

"Friends of mine," Cirella said, sitting down in a chair.

"I know. You guys pull any jobs lately?"

"Jobs?"

"Yeah, you know, you knock anyone over lately?"

Cirella curled his lips. "Nah, not us. We're out of the business now. Have been ever since we got out of prison."

Downing couldn't help but laugh. "Is that so? What about Danny Falk? That's not what he says."

"Yeah, well, as I'm sure you know since you interviewed him this morning, Danny's not entirely stable. He says a lot of things that don't have any validity to them."

"How'd you know we talked to him this morning?"

"I know a lot of things."

"So it appears. How exactly does that happen?"

"You know how it is," Cirella answered. "You just happen to know people who know things. Little nuggets of information float in the air, and you just grab them and pull them down."

"Kind of like us raiding your storage unit, huh?"

"What storage unit?"

"The one you were sitting outside of watching us."

"Oh, that, you mean when I just happened to pull over to the side of the road so I could light my cigarette?"

Downing grinned. The man had an answer for everything. "And you wouldn't know anything about the fact you stored stuff inside there, huh?"

"I can honestly say I know nothing about it. Did you check who the owner of the unit was according to the records?"

"We did. Came back to an Alfred Morris."

"Well, then he's probably the guy you're looking for."

"We don't think so," Downing said. "We think this Morris is an alias for someone else. Someone who's too smart to leave his own name."

"Could be. There's a lot of crafty people out there."

"There certainly is."

"By the way, should we be doing this downtown or something? Someplace more official?" Cirella gave off a smug aura, knowing he was untouchable.

"No, this is fine. You're not under arrest or anything, at least not yet."

"Well, you'll let me know when we are, right?"

"You'll be the first to know." Downing then smiled. "You'll probably know as soon as the arrest warrant's typed out, huh?"

"That's possible."

"Maybe it's that Mark guy that Falk told us about. Maybe he's the one you get all your information from."

"I don't know anyone named Mark," Cirella said. He then looked to his friends. "You guys know someone named Mark?" Rollins and Brantly both shook their heads in unison. Cirella then looked back to the lieutenant. "Sorry. They don't know anyone named Mark either."

"What about Montgomery?"

"Who?"

"Montgomery," Downing repeated. "You know, the

guy you knocked over and killed a few days ago, robbed him, took his jewelry and stuff."

"Sorry, someone else did that one."

"Not according to the information we have."

"What information is that? You got fingerprints?"

"Maybe."

Cirella laughed. "If you had fingerprints, we wouldn't be sitting here talking. We'd be in handcuffs. Maybe you got some kind of picture, video, security camera, something like that?"

"We're working on it."

"Well, you keep doing that, maybe you'll eventually get somewhere with it."

"Maybe we have an eyewitness?" Downing said.

"Oh yeah? That's great. But wait, didn't the guy get killed?"

"There was a guard there."

"Outstanding. Maybe he saw the whole thing go down, huh?"

Downing grinned, knowing this line of questioning wasn't going to get him anywhere. Not that he really expected it to. It was more of a session to get familiar with his targets, hoping to find some nugget of information as to how they operated, their line of thinking, maybe even a slip of the tongue that they could use to nab them later. Unfortunately, Cirella didn't seem to be the kind of man who slipped up very often. He was ready for the cat-and-mouse game.

Gruber and Cirella then engaged in a few questions, giving Downing a chance to move his eyes around the room, hoping something would jump out at him. It was a very basic apartment. No pictures on the walls or tables, no personality, everything was very bland. It didn't look like an apartment that someone called home. It was more of a place of someone who didn't plan to stay long and just wanted something basic that they could pack up real quick if they needed to.

"No family?" Downing asked.

"What's that?"

Downing then pointed at the walls. "No pictures. Wife, kids, nothing?"

"I'm not married," Cirella said.

"Divorced?"

"Never been."

"Too bad. Kids?"

"Never had the time."

"Too bad," Downing said. "You don't know what you're missing until you go through a divorce."

"You?"

Downing laughed. "Oh yeah. About six years now."

"Rough."

"It was bound to happen."

"How's that?" Cirella asked.

"She didn't like that I was already married. To the job. She always took a back seat. Married for five years to a detective who pays more attention to his work than to her must have felt like a hundred."

"Sounds like you're a guy who needs to take a few steps back, reevaluate your priorities."

Downing laughed again. "A lot of people would think so. I'm too set in my ways though. I love my job. Love putting bad guys away, getting them off the street. Everything else takes a backseat to that."

"You're an asset to the city. We should have a hundred more like you."

"What about you? Ever think about settling down? Buy a house, have some kids?"

"Nah, that's a dream life for other people, not for me. I'm too much of a loner. I like my space. I like being able to do what I want without asking someone else for permission."

"I understand completely."

"Is there anything else I can do for you?" Cirella asked. "Would you like a drink? Sit down? Anything?"

"No, thank you. I just wanted to stop by, introduce myself to you, ask you a few questions."

"Well, I'm glad you did. It was nice getting to know you."

"I'm sure we'll be seeing a lot more of each other," Downing said.

"I wouldn't count on that," Cirella said.

"Don't think so?"

"You're after bad guys, right? That's obviously nobody in this room."

"You guys all got records."

"In the past," Cirella replied.

"What about the future? I don't see any of you guys working at Walmart or anything."

"We pick up an odd job here or there. All legit."

"I'm sure you do. Before we go, I just wanna leave you with some lasting thoughts."

"OK?"

"We'll be watching you guys closely from here on out," Downing said. "You might not see us, but we'll be there, waiting for one of you to slip up. And when you do, then we won't need your ex-partner for anything."

"There's a reason he's an ex-partner."

"I'm sure there is. Be that as it may, I'll be there the next time you try to pull a job, waiting for that slip-up."

"Won't happen."

"Maybe. Maybe not. But you better believe we'll be there. And I'll put you all back in prison."

"Not me."

"What, you think you're above it all? You can't be caught? The best criminals in the history of the world, they all got caught at one point."

"Well, we both know that's not exactly true. History is littered with people who got away with their crimes all the time. If no mistakes are made, they won't be caught. And there's nothing you can do about it."

"Except putting you away."

Cirella grinned, appreciating the detective's determination. He stood back up in anticipation of them leaving soon. "Listen, I ain't ever going back to prison. If you're ever right about that slip-up, you better come ready for a fight, 'cause I will die in a hail of bullets on a street corner before I ever see the inside of a jail cell again."

"Is that a promise?"

Cirella shrugged. "It just is what it is."

"I'll remember that."

"I hope you do."

"So you're saying I should be wearing a vest the next time I see you?"

"It probably would be a good life choice," Cirella said with a smile. "That way you get to live to see that next divorce of yours."

"You know, I don't like what you do, but I almost like you. I'll almost hate having to take you down. Almost."

"I guess that would make two of us."

"I'll be seein' ya."

Downing tapped his partner and the two of them walked out the door. Cirella waited a few minutes then walked over to the door and opened it, taking a peek out in the hallway to make sure that they'd gone. He saw them step into the elevator, then he went back inside his apartment.

"They're gonna be all over us like a cheap suit," Rollins said.

Cirella put his hand up, appearing to not be worried at all. "Relax. This will work out perfectly for us."

"How so?"

"They're gonna be so eager to take us down that they won't even see us slipping away right under their noses."

Once the detectives got back in their car, they started discussing what was said in the apartment.

"What do you think?" Gruber asked. "Cirella's a very confident guy."

"And with good reason. They're good and they know it."

"You think they got another job lined up?"

"Ehh, tough to say. I didn't really notice anything that would suggest it going either way. We'll stay on them."

"They're not gonna try and pull something if they know we're watching."

"I dunno about that," Downing said. "This crew's so good, so confident, that they might get a kick out of trying to pull something off while we're right up their ass. If they do, we need to be ready."

14

As soon as Carter was finished work, he drove straight home, hoping to hash things out with his wife again. Before leaving for work in the morning, he tried to have another conversation with her, but Stacy gave him the cold shoulder. Usually, she tried to have breakfast ready for him before he left for work, even if it was something as simple as a bagel with cream cheese. This morning, though, there was nothing. She sat at the table with the kids and didn't say one word to him. Jack tried to steal a kiss from her before he left, but she resisted, not even letting him kiss her cheek.

When Carter pulled into the driveway, he could tell right away something was wrong. Stacy's car wasn't there. She and the kids were always there, waiting for him to get home. If for some reason she had to go somewhere, she'd always send him a text or call him to let him know. He double-checked his phone to make sure he didn't miss something. Carter walked into the house, and right away, he missed the sounds that usually accompanied him when he got home. The sound of the kids playing, the kids' TV shows that were usually on, toys that lit up and made sounds, none of that was present now. It was deathly quiet.

It was weird not getting a kiss from his beautiful wife when he got home, he thought as he started moving throughout the house, not sure what he was looking for since it was obvious they weren't home. He hoped that maybe he'd find some type of sign or clue as to why they weren't there or where they'd gone. After looking in their bedroom, then the living room and the bathroom, he finally found what he was looking for. Right there on the kitchen table, there was a note. With trepidation, he picked it up and started reading it. It was exactly what he feared it would be.

Jack, I'm sorry, but I just couldn't stay right now. I took the kids to my parents' house and I'll be staying there for a little while. I'm not sure when or if we'll be back. I just need time to think. I know you're doing what you think you have to do and what's necessary for us, but I just don't agree, not to the degree that you're doing it. Even if everything works out the way you think it will, that money still isn't ours. We didn't earn it. Can we really live with ourselves knowing we took money off of someone else? I'm not sure that's how I want to live. I won't tell my parents about any of this. I'll just say we had an argument. Maybe we can talk again in a few days. Stacy.

Carter sighed as he let his arms fall down to his side. He looked around the kitchen, though he didn't focus on anything in particular. He was just thinking about how much he had bungled everything. He was only throwing in with Cirella again to help his family, and now his family was leaving him because of it. He wasn't sure what the right thing to do was anymore. All he knew was he couldn't back out of the job he already agreed to with Cirella. Though they were on good terms, he didn't know how Cirella and the old crew would take it if he suddenly withdrew at the last minute after already saying he would do it. He already knew the details of the job, which he knew was a strike against him if he wanted to call it quits. Even if they thought Carter could be trusted to keep quiet, they wouldn't like him walking around knowing about the job if he didn't participate in it. He'd be what was considered a loose end. At this point, he figured it was probably best to just go through with the job and hope Stacy would soften her stance later. Hopefully it wouldn't be much later.

Faced with the unpleasant task of facing the rest of the night alone, Carter sent a text to Cirella to let him know his nights were now completely free for the next few days. He knew they had to go over plans at some point, so no time like the present. Almost immediately, Cirella sent him a text back, asking him to meet at a restaurant for dinner. Since there was nothing, or no one there to stop him, Carter agreed. He got dressed, then drove down to the restaurant to meet Cirella about thirty minutes after the initial text.

Cirella and the rest of the gang were already at the restaurant waiting for Carter. As soon as their guest sat down at the table, they told him about the police being on their tail. They wanted to make sure Carter was ready for it in case the cops knocked on his door one day. Little did they know that knock would come sooner rather than later.

Downing and Gruber were sitting outside the restaurant and taking a close look at everybody who walked in. Every face that looked even a little familiar, and those that didn't, were immediately investigated. Gruber had his laptop out and fired up with Cirella's file open, trying to match up anyone who even had a remote history with Cirella. Anybody who was known to have any type of relationship with him, all the way back to the day he graduated high school, was listed.

"Get anything on that last guy who walked in?" Downing asked.

"Not yet," Gruber said. "Still searching. You know, they might not be here to meet anybody. Could just be leading us on a wild goose chase, wanting to make us do extra work."

"Possibility."

"But you still think they're meeting someone?"

"I don't really know. They're a man short on their

crew. Maybe they can operate with three. Maybe they want another guy. Maybe they're just here having dinner, maybe they like to eat out a lot, I don't know. Anything could be possible with these guys."

Another minute went by, though Gruber kept searching, finally finding something. "Wait a minute. Yeah, here we go."

"You got something?" Downing asked, leaning over from the driver's side to see what his partner had come up with.

Gruber turned his laptop to the side so his boss could get a better look. "This looks like the guy, doesn't it?"

"That's him. Who is it?"

Gruber spun the laptop back towards him so he could read the information better. "Jack Carter."

"Carter. Why's that name sound familiar?"

"Because he is a former member of Cirella's crew."

"Former member? I remember seeing something about that. Refresh my memory."

"Apparently he was a part of the crew for several years, then he broke off with them when the rest of them were sent to prison."

"He never went, though?" Downing asked.

"No. They apparently didn't have anything on him at the time and the others never flipped, so he walked."

"These guys don't flip on their own."

"Falk?"

"I don't consider Falk really to be one of them. Anyway, Falk was this guy's replacement?"

"Yeah."

"Seems they took a step down," Downing said. "What else we got on this guy?"

"Nothing."

"What do you mean nothing? We got nothing? How can we have nothing?"

"Because we got nothing," Gruber replied. "He's kept a low profile, nothing in here about being a suspect in anything, appears like he's turned his life around."

"Are you serious?"

"He's apparently married now, couple kids, says he's working in construction. That's what the report says from the last detectives who checked the group out."

Downing grumbled a little.

"What, you don't think so?" Gruber asked.

"These guys don't change their stripes. They don't change who they are at their core. They alter their paths sometimes, but they don't change completely."

Gruber laughed. "Maybe this guy found true love. You know what they say about the love of a good woman."

"Did he marry Mother Teresa?"

"Man, you and love are a cynical pair."

"You haven't gotten married yet. Believe me, take it

from someone who knows, you'll be there in twenty years too."

"I would like to believe it's possible for someone like that to find someone special and change who they are."

"You're a hopeless romantic at heart," Downing said.

"Hey, maybe you'll change your tune the next time you get married."

Downing scoffed at the suggestion. "Pfft. Like that's happening again. Believe me, I am never walking down that aisle again."

"So, what do you think? Think this guy's joining the crew again?"

Downing nodded. "I think that's a good conclusion."

"Maybe they're just having dinner. Catching up on old times. Maybe they've stayed in touch over the years?"

"You know I don't believe in coincidences. They boot Falk out of the group, then all of a sudden, this guy shows up out of the blue? No, I think this is a business meeting. Maybe they needed another guy for an upcoming job. Who better to go to than someone you already know and trust? Someone who's been there before."

"If they're going back to him then he must be pretty good too."

"I would say so."

"Maybe we should talk to his wife," Gruber said. "She might be able to give us a clue as to what he's up to."

"Possible. We'll stay here for a little while, see if anyone else shows up."

"You think they're waiting for someone else?"

"Hard to say. Let's give it another thirty minutes."

"And then what?"

"And then we'll go inside and have a little chat with them again," Downing said. "Maybe we can rattle a few cages. We'll focus on Carter. He's got something the rest of them don't have."

"What's that?"

"A family."

The detectives waited another thirty minutes, still checking the faces of people going into the restaurant, though nobody else had ties with Cirella that they could find. They figured Carter was it.

"Let's go," Downing said.

"What are we gonna do?"

"I dunno. We'll just wing it and see what happens."

Gruber rolled his eyes as the two of them got out of the car. He hated that strategy. He liked to prepare, liked to know what they were walking into. Downing, though, was the complete opposite. He had no problem walking into a situation and flying by the seat of his pants. He found that he sometimes got results that way. Sometimes they ran into problems as a result of it too, but he always thought it was worth the risk.

He liked to be proactive and spur something on as a result of his actions rather than just sit back and hope that something might happen.

Once the detectives walked into the restaurant, they immediately located the table with their suspects. Of course, they were spotted too as they walked towards it.

"Oh no," Rollins said, observing the two police officers.

"What?" Brantly asked, turning his head, along with the rest of the crew to see what their partner was referring to.

"We got company. And it's not the good kind."

They turned their heads back around as they waited for the detectives to get to them. They looked down at the table and waited silently.

"Who's this?" Carter quietly asked.

"Police," Rollins answered. "The ones we were telling you about."

"Well, well, well," Downing said with a swagger. "Mr. Cirella and crew." Downing and Gruber grabbed empty chairs from nearby tables and put them at the end of the booth, joining the crew.

"What a surprise to see you here," Cirella replied.

"Isn't it? Amazing how we keep running into each other."

"Sure is."

"What do we have here?" Downing asked, looking

at Carter. "You expanding operations right under our noses? Adding to the troops?"

"He's just a friend. Haven't seen him in a while."

"Oh, I'm well aware of who you are, Mr. Carter."

Carter looked at him, surprised that he knew who he was.

"What are you doing here with these guys?" Downing asked.

"He's just having dinner with some old friends," Cirella replied.

"How 'bout you let him talk? He can talk, right?" Downing then looked at Carter again, getting a little cocky. "You can talk, right?"

"Yeah," Carter answered.

"See, there you go." Downing looked around the table. "Told you he could talk. So, what are you doing here?"

"Like he said, just eating."

"Your wife know you're here partying it up with these guys, these convicted felons?"

"She knows."

"And she's OK with that? You supposedly cleaned up your life, got away from these punks, started a family, and for some strange reason, here you are, back with this crew again. How do you explain that?"

"It's just dinner."

"Let me give you some advice before it's too late. If you are thinking about hooking up with these guys again because maybe you miss the rush of pulling off a job, maybe for old-time's sake, or maybe you just need the money, I'd seriously reconsider your options. Because I'm onto these guys. And whatever job they got coming up, I'm gonna be there. And if that means putting everyone away in a cell, or putting them six feet under, if I were you, I'd think about what that would do to your family."

Carter looked at him and nodded. "Noted."

"Why would you wanna hook up with these guys again, anyway?"

"It's just dinner."

"So that's the story you're gonna stick with, huh?"

"It's the truth."

"We'll see about that."

"You wanna join us?" Cirella asked. "We'll get you a menu."

"No thanks, I'm good." Downing then looked away for a second, getting a smile on his face like he just figured out a puzzle, then slapped his hand down on the table. "I know what this is. This is like the last supper, right? The last big meal before you all get thrown in the clink?"

Cirella smirked, appreciating the man's boastfulness. "Maybe it's a victory celebration."

"Victory? What kind of victory?"

"Maybe we already pulled off a job right under your nose?"

Downing grinned, also appreciating his opponent's sense of humor. "That would be worth celebrating. I know that didn't happen, but it's nice to dream, isn't it?"

"Maybe it won't be a dream."

"What? So you're admitting you're setting something up right in front of me?"

"Listen, whether I admit anything or not, you already think you know what's going on here. Nothing I say is gonna change that. You already think we're gonna pull off a job soon, so whatever we say really has no bearing on that."

"You're right about that. I just figured coming here, I would re-emphasize that I'm watching. I'm gonna be there. And you're gonna go down."

"Well, I guess we'll see about that."

"There is an alternative," Downing said.

"Oh yeah? What's that?"

"You and your crew go home, cancel whatever it is that you're planning, and you start living useful, law-abiding lives. Then neither of us ever has to worry about the other one again."

Cirella looked at his partners and smiled. "I'm not worried. Do I look worried?"

"No, you don't. And that's kind of troubling."

"It should be."

"Not for me," Downing said. "It's troubling for you."

"I guess I just don't see it that way."

"Well, maybe it's time you start changing your outlook on things."

"I think I'm good the way I am. So is it always gonna be you two outside watching?" Cirella asked. "Or you guys gonna switch it up sometimes?"

"Oh, we'll switch it up."

"I'm sure you will. How come you never let him do any of the talking?" Cirella pointed at Gruber. "How come you take up all the air?"

Downing briefly looked at his partner before answering. "Oh, he's more the strong silent type. Man of few words. I'm more the loudmouth."

"Every team's gotta have one, right?"

"So who's the loudmouth in your group? The one you just can't keep under control? You?"

Cirella shook his head. "You already arrested him."

"Oh, sorry about that. You want him back?"

"No apologies necessary. And believe me, you can keep him."

"Speaking of that, Falk never did tell me why you kicked him out. Just said you had disagreements. What happened with him?"

"The honest truth?"

"Sure," Downing replied. "Let's give that a shot."

"Honestly, he was a liability. Didn't do what he was asked, didn't do what he was told, didn't fall in line, was a wild card, and I never knew what he was gonna do at any given moment, was a hothead, did things that weren't necessary. I can keep going, but I'm sure you don't have all night."

"That's kind of funny. He said some of those same things about you."

Cirella snickered. "Do I seem like I'm any of those things?"

"No, you do not."

"That's right, 'cause I'm not.

The two groups sat there staring at each other for another minute, both sides having said everything they wanted to. Downing then pushed his chair out and stood up, followed by Gruber.

"Well, I guess that'll do it for now," Downing said.

"Sure you don't want a cocktail or something?" Cirella asked. "It'll be my treat."

"No thank you. Gotta keep my eyes clear and focused."

"Ah, that's right. You don't want your head foggy and miss us robbing a bank while you're snoozing it off."

The detectives started to leave, but before doing so, Downing tapped Carter on the arm. "Remember what I said, kid. Don't do something to your family that you'll regret."

"I'll remember," Carter replied.

15

After leaving the restaurant and feeling like Carter getting thrown into the mix was a wild card, Downing had another detective stake out his house too. He also had another team following Cirella, to replace him so he and Gruber could get a good night's sleep, feeling like they would need it. He had a feeling they were in store for something big in the next few days. Whatever Cirella was planning, Downing didn't think it was going to take very long. Certainly not weeks or months. He was thinking days, maybe a week at the most. It just felt like something was about to go down. And when he got those feelings, those hunches, he was usually right.

As soon as Downing got up the next morning, he checked in with both teams. The one following Cirella reported nothing unusual. After leaving the restaurant, Cirella went straight to his apartment and stayed there the rest of the night. The team on Carter's house, though, reported back with something interesting. They told Downing that they didn't think anybody was there. They saw Carter come home. They saw Carter leave again for work in the morning. But there was no sign of anybody else. They even knocked on the door without getting an answer. Wherever Carter's wife and kids were, the detectives didn't think they were living together.

After getting to the office and digging into the background of Carter and his wife, they discovered Stacy's parents lived about two hours away. They had the local police department do a drive-by with one of their patrol cars to see if Stacy's car was there. Once the police positively identified that the car was indeed there, Downing and Gruber quickly packed up their things to hit the road, wanting to make sure they got to the parents' house before Stacy left. Something told them that they wouldn't have to worry about it. Considering Stacy and the kids weren't at their own house that morning, or the previous night, it was a sign that they were having a prolonged visit at Stacy's parents.

The detectives arrived at Stacy's parents' home about fifteen minutes ahead of schedule, finding the traffic fairly light for that time of the morning. Her car was still there, parked behind a van in the double wide driveway. As Gruber grabbed his files, he bemoaned the length of the drive.

"Hope this trip wasn't for nothing. She might not even talk to us."

"We'll just have to make sure that she does," Downing said.

"Easier said than done."

"This woman's not a criminal or a shady character. She has no criminal history of any kind, not even a speeding or parking ticket. She has kids, she'll want to protect them."

"She also has a husband," Gruber said. "She might want to protect him too."

"Guess we'll see."

The pair got out of the house and approached the two-story brick colonial.

"Looks like a nice place," Downing said, passing by a nicely maintained flower garden.

"Yeah, not too bad."

After knocking on the door, a middle-aged woman quickly answered. She appeared to be in a jovial mood from the smile and expression on her face, probably because her daughter and grandchildren were there.

"Yes? Can I help you?"

"Uhh, yes, ma'am," Downing said. "We were hoping to talk to Stacy Carter, I understand she's here."

"Can I ask who you are and what you want her for?"

"Well, we're, uhh... acquaintances of her husband, Jack."

A concerned look suddenly came across the

woman's face. "Is everything OK? Is something wrong?"

"Oh, no, no, no, everything's fine, ma'am," Downing said, trying not to get anyone's emotions up. He wanted everyone to stay even-keel, like they weren't even there.

"What do you want Stacy for?"

"Well, it's a private matter, ma'am. Would you mind getting her for us? It really is important."

"Well, all right, wait here."

The woman closed the door, then retreated back into the house to inform her daughter that she had visitors. Downing turned to his partner and gave him a shrug, putting his hands in his pockets as they waited.

"What do you think?" Gruber asked.

"I think she's going to get her daughter."

"I know that. I mean, do you think she suspects something?"

"Wouldn't you?" Downing replied. "Couple strange men, who look like cops, show up at your door, looking for your daughter and saying we know her husband. What would you think?"

"I'd think something's up."

"All we can do is try to make it as casual as possible."

A few seconds later the door opened up again. This time it was Stacy. She was easily recognizable from the photo they had of her. She looked exactly the same. Though now thirty, Stacy still had a youthful appearance, looking like she was ten years younger than she was.

"Can I help you?" Stacy asked, looking at the two investigators with equal amounts of nervous anxiety and distrust.

Downing reached into his pocket and pulled out his badge to show her, keeping it low and palmed inside his hand as if he was trying to shield it from anyone else who may have had some prying eyes.

"Lieutenant Downing, ma'am. This is Detective Gruber. I was wondering if we could talk to you for a minute."

"What about?"

Just before Downing was about to speak, one of her kids made themselves visible behind her.

"You might feel more comfortable speaking about this privately."

Stacy turned around and saw her child standing there. "Just a moment," she told the detectives. She then left them and picked her child up, taking him to his grandmother. She came back to the front door and stepped outside, closing the door behind them.

"What's this about?" Stacy asked.

Downing looked around the porch, wanting to make it as easy and comfortable for her as possible. He saw a bench seat along the house with a wicker chair across from it. "Can we sit?"

"Sure."

Stacy sat on the bench, Downing sitting next to her,

though not too close so he didn't freak her out or make her uncomfortable. Gruber took the wicker chair.

"We wanted to talk to you about your husband," Downing said.

"Why? What's happened?"

"Well, nothing's happened yet. We want to make sure it remains that way."

"I don't understand."

"Are you and your husband still living together?" Gruber asked.

"Yes, of course. Why?"

"We understand you weren't at your house last night or this morning. We were just wondering why."

"I don't see why that's any of your concern."

Sensing she was starting to get defensive and they might lose her, Downing tried to ease up on questioning her whereabouts, not wanting it to sound like they were investigating her.

"Here's our interest, ma'am," Downing said. "We arrested a man named Danny Falk the other day. Have you ever heard of him?"

Stacy thought for a minute, but the name didn't ring a bell. "No, I haven't. Who is he?"

"Well, that's not really important to the story. What is important is how he connects to your husband."

"Jack has never mentioned that name before."

"And I believe that," Downing replied. "Unfortunately, Falk connects to another man your husband might know, a Dominic Cirella."

Stacy wanted to just close her eyes and crawl up into a ball and close herself off upon hearing that name. But she knew she had to try to keep a straight face and pretend like it didn't bother her.

"Do you know Cirella, ma'am?"

Stacy sighed deeply before answering, not wanting to lie about it. "Yes."

"You do?"

"Well, yeah, I mean, I know of him. We're not friends or anything."

"And Jack?"

"What's this about, Detective?"

"Isaac Brantly and Noah Rollins," Downing said. "You and your husband know those names too?"

Stacy sighed again, not thrilled with the line of questioning. "If we're done here, I'd like to get back inside and tend to my children."

Before Stacy could stand up, Downing put his hand out to prevent her from leaving.

"Ma'am, just give me a minute, please. We're not here to hurt you or your husband. In fact, if we can, we're here to help you."

"How so?" Stacy asked.

"First, you do know those names, do you not?"

Stacy groaned, not wanting to look back on the past, or even admit that it happened. "Yes. I'm sure you already know my husband was involved with that group a long time ago."

"And then you came into the picture and swept him away from all that, right?" Downing said.

Stacy shrugged. "He hasn't been involved with them."

"And I believe that. I do. What I'm trying to prevent is him swaying off that straight line that you put him on."

"He hasn't lost his way if that's what you're thinking."

"I hope not. But in our investigation on Falk, we discovered he was one of Cirella's crew members. For some reason or another, they had a falling out. Anyway, we believe Cirella is about to go on another job soon. We've been following the crew for a couple days now."

"What's this have to do with Jack?"

"Last night, we followed Cirella to a restaurant. The other members of the team were there. Then, after half an hour, another man showed up. That man turned out to be your husband."

"So, what are you saying?"

"I'm asking. Is your husband mixed up with this crew again?"

Stacy took another deep breath. Downing could see her arms start to shake slightly, though she got it under control rather quickly.

"No, he's not," Stacy replied.

"Are you sure?" Gruber asked. "Because it certainly does appear to be the case."

"No, Jack wouldn't get mixed up with them again. He's committed to his family now."

"Which one?" Downing asked. "His former family? Or the one including you and the kids?"

"Us."

"Then what was he doing at that restaurant?"

Even though Stacy was staunchly opposed to what her husband was doing, she wasn't about to give him up to the police. She was doing everything in her power to keep him out of trouble, and admitting that Jack was getting in bed with his former colleagues again didn't seem like a good idea, even if they did say they were trying to help. Helping him into prison, she thought.

"When was the last time you saw Cirella or the others?" Downing asked.

Stacy thought for a moment, wanting to be as truthful as possible without hurting Jack. "He stopped by the house a few days ago."

"Why?"

"My husband and I have been going through some rough times financially. Last week, we noticed that all of our bills had been paid off, even ones that we'd been behind on."

"Cirella?"

"Yes."

"So he paid off your bills, hoping that'd get him in good with Jack again, thinking he'd rejoin the team? Make him feel guilty or something?"

"I guess, I don't know."

"So is he rejoining the team?"

"First off," Stacy said. "I'm just here for a few days to visit my parents. They haven't seen the kids for a while. It's not for any other reason you're thinking."

"OK. Why would Jack go to that restaurant last night then?"

"Since I wasn't home, he was just going to have dinner with them, I guess catch up on old times. They haven't seen each other in a while, but they were always on good terms. But Jack was also going to tell them that whatever they were planning, he wasn't getting involved in it. That's not his life anymore."

Downing and Gruber looked at each other, not sure if they believed that.

"Are you sure about that?" Downing asked.

"Yes. We talked about it."

"You talked about it? Do you know exactly what Cirella was planning?"

"No," Stacy answered. "Jack said he only talked in general terms, not wanting to get specific unless Jack agreed to go in on the deal."

"So Cirella is definitely planning something?"

"As far as I know."

"But you, or Jack, don't know the details?"

"Yep."

"So Jack was only at the restaurant last night as a courtesy, and to let his friends know he wasn't coming back in?" Downing asked.

"That's right."

They talked for a few more minutes, but the detectives didn't get anything they could consider useful. It was clear that Stacy wasn't going to come off her stance that her husband wasn't involved in anything. They couldn't tell at that point whether she was deliberately lying to protect him, whether she really believed it, or whether she might have actually been telling the truth.

"Well, we're gonna get going here," Downing said, slapping both his knees before standing up. "Thank you for talking to us and for your honesty."

Stacy gave a half-hearted smile and shook the detective's hand. "Thanks."

Downing and Gruber then walked back to their car.

"What do you think?" Gruber asked.

"I don't know."

"Sounded like she was telling the truth."

"Could be."

"You don't think so?"

"To be perfectly honest, I'm not really sure what to believe right now," Downing said. "I believe it's possible she's telling the truth. I also believe it's possible she's lying to protect her husband."

"What now?"

"Right now, hope that one of them slips up somewhere."

16

There were only two days to go before the armored car robbery was supposed to take place. As he usually did, Cirella had to go to Mark's house to go over any last-minute details or changes in the operation. Before doing that, however, he had to lose his tail. Brantly and Rollins reported that they weren't being followed, so they decided to use that to their advantage. They only had to lose one car right now. Brantly and Cirella were the same height and had a similar build, so they figured they could switch places to throw the cops off who were watching Cirella's apartment.

Rollins and Brantly pulled into the parking lot in one car. The detectives staking it out watched the pair walk to the entrance door. Rollins and Brantly both had on baseball hats and sunglasses, looking like they were trying to keep from getting noticed.

"Who do these guys think they are?" a detective said with a laugh. "They really think those getups are gonna slip by us or something?"

"Maybe these guys aren't as smart as everything thinks they are," his partner replied.

Once Rollins and Brantly got inside Cirella's apartment, Brantly and Cirella switched clothes.

"You really think this is gonna work?" Rollins asked.

"It'll work," Cirella replied. "Two guys walk in, dressed a certain way, those same two guys, in the same clothes, walk back out. Who's gonna think any different? Besides, I'll be on the inside of you, so you'll be the one they get the better look at. They'll just assume everything's the same."

"I hope you're right."

"It'll work. Trust me. Besides, they're cops, how bright can they be? If they were smart, they wouldn't be cops."

The men laughed. "Yeah, that's true."

They didn't want to give the appearance that something was up by leaving right away, wanting to make sure it seemed like a regular, normal visit, so they stayed inside the apartment for over thirty minutes.

"Just sit tight until I get back," Cirella said. "There's food in the fridge if you get hungry or anything."

"I'll be fine," Brantly replied, plopping down on the couch with a magazine.

Cirella and Rollins left the apartment. Once

outside, Cirella made sure he was on the inside of Rollins, making sure his face was obscured by Rollins' body.

"There they go again," the detective remarked. He laughed once more. "Who do these guys think they are? Movie stars? They look like they're trying to hide out from the paparazzi or something."

Cirella successfully remained hidden behind Rollins until they got to the car, Cirella quickly jumping into the driver's seat first. Once Rollins got in, they peeled out of the parking lot.

"Tools," the detective said. "These idiots think they're big stuff or something. Hope they enjoy their last few days of freedom."

WHEN CIRELLA and Rollins arrived at Mark's home, he was already outside waiting for them. Though Rollins and Mark had met several times before, it was only the second time Rollins had ever been to the house. Mark walked up to the car as the two men got out.

"Sure you weren't tailed?" Mark asked.

"Don't sweat it," Cirella answered. "Those idiots think I'm still back at my apartment. Switched clothes with Isaac, so no need to worry."

"Good. Let's go inside and talk."

They went inside to their usual spot after

exchanging greetings with Mark's wife on the way and immediately got down to business.

"I'm a little worried about everything right now," Mark said.

"Everything's under control," Cirella replied.

"I'm hearing the heat's on you pretty good."

Cirella threw one of his arms up and made a condescending face like he wasn't very concerned. "It's nothing."

"Downing's a good detective. I've looked at his record and it's very good. He doesn't miss often."

"Well, he's missing here."

"I just wanna make sure the heat isn't too hot right now," Mark said. "'Cause if it is, I don't wanna jeopardize this job. I can hand this off to someone else, and I'll give you the next one down the line when the heat loosens up."

"Everything's fine. They're not even tailing all of us right now, only me."

"Probably know nothing gets done without you."

"Even so, that still gives us plenty of room."

"You gonna be able to lose them?"

"When the time comes, I'll lose them," Cirella answered. "Believe me, I'm not even a little worried about these clowns. If they really knew something, they'd be blanketing all of us all the time. What it says to me is that they don't really know anything and are just hoping one of us does something stupid."

"Yeah, that kind of jives with what I've been hearing. Without having a credible piece of information to act on, they don't have the manpower to follow each of you around separately for who knows how long. That's why they're just limiting it to you."

"Believe me, I'll be able to lose these guys with my eyes closed. Don't even give it a second thought."

"You're sure?"

"No question."

"All right, then, I'll trust you on it," Mark said. "What about Carter?"

"He's in."

"You're sure you can count on him?"

"Wouldn't have asked him if I wasn't," Cirella replied. "He's been out of the game a while, yeah, but you don't just lose the qualities that made you good to begin with. He'll be fine. I have no concerns about him."

"Good to hear."

"What I do have concerns with are the men you're using to block traffic. Reliable?"

"I've used them all before. Not on big jobs, but they're all capable of doing this. They'll be there. The north side of the street will be blocked off half an hour before the armored car is scheduled to get there. On the south side, they'll start blocking traffic a few minutes before, redirecting everyone to that side street that runs just before it. They won't let anyone through except the armored car and you guys."

"OK, good. I know we were originally talking about

waiting next to the semi in our car and then waiting for the armored car to get there, but I think it'd be better for us to be behind the armored car as we drive, that way they don't get hinky, wondering why there's no other cars on the road besides them."

As the men were sketching things out on a piece of paper, Rollins saw one potential issue. "Don't you think they're gonna notice that every car gets redirected except for them? That's a big red flag."

Cirella and Mark looked at each other, thinking that he had a point. Cirella then shook his head, knowing what to do. "No, here's what we do. We block the north end of the street completely, just as we said." Cirella continued to doodle on the paper to help explain his point. "On the south end, we don't block it completely. We just keep letting cars through."

"That's gonna throw things off," Mark said.

"No, it'll be fine. We just stop traffic a few cars at a time, letting them through the south end. When they get to the north end, those guys keep letting them pass through. Those guys at the north end, they don't let anyone in, but they'll let cars out. The guys on the south end let a few cars go at a time until the armored car gets there. If we're behind the armored car, then they let the armored car and us go through, and that's it. They block everything after us. Then it's just us two on the road. When Isaac sees the car, he plows it, with us coming up behind it. Then me and Noah pull up and jump out, blow the back door, grab the money, then we're out within a few minutes. We exit on the north side and we're good."

The three men glanced at each other, all of them nodding.

"That'll work," Rollins said.

"All right, I'll let the other boys know the plan so they're on board," Mark replied.

"You're sure they're good?" Cirella asked.

"Trust me, I wouldn't use them if I wasn't sure."

"OK. Your word's good enough."

"Let's get it done. It's a big payday for all of us."

"We need to make sure we can all communicate out there, even those guys blocking traffic, just in case something happens, we can get a warning out."

Mark got up from his chair and walked over to his bookcase, taking a box off one of the shelves. He brought it back to the table and opened it, revealing several two-way radios.

"You guys take one," Mark said. "Keep it on you while you're pulling the job. I'll give one to each of the other teams on both sides of the street. That way if something goes wrong, you'll be ready for it."

Satisfied, Cirella picked a radio up and put it in his pocket. With their meeting done, Cirella and Rollins walked back to their car. Before getting in, they stood at their respective doors and talked over the car.

"What do you think?" Rollins asked. "Should go off without a hitch, right?"

"As long as those guys do their jobs and block traffic, yeah, should go off without a hitch."

"And if they don't?"

"Then things will get more interesting," Cirella said.

"What if a cop shows up? What if Downing and his guys are there? What if we can't lose them?"

"We'll lose them."

"How? How we gonna do that?"

"Just leave it to me. I'll take care of it. I've got some ideas."

17

Carter had just walked through the door when his phone started ringing. He assumed it was Cirella with more instructions on the job they were about to pull. He was pleasantly surprised to see that it wasn't him. It was Stacy.

"Hey," Jack said softly.

"Hey. Home from work yet?"

"Yeah, I just walked in."

"Good. I was trying to wait until you were done."

"When you coming home, Stace?"

"I don't know. I just want... just tell me you're not going to do that job, and I'll be home tonight."

"You know I can't do that."

"I don't care about the money," Stacy said. "I don't care about anything else. I just want you safe and at home with us. Not pulling some job that might get you killed or locked up. I don't care how much money it is. It's not worth it."

"I've already agreed. I can't back out now."

Stacy knew it was a lost cause and not worth pleading anymore.

"How are the kids?" Jack asked. "I miss them."

"They're good. My parents are having a good time with them."

"I miss you too."

"I miss you too, Jack. I don't want to be apart."

"Then don't. Come back home."

"I can't just sit there and wait and pray that something doesn't happen to you when I know you're out there. I can't do that."

"Well, it's gonna be the same thing there," Jack said.

"No. At least here I have my parents to talk to, to try and take my mind off things."

"What about work? You're gonna miss a couple shifts."

"I've already called out for the week," Stacy said. "Told them one of the kids was sick."

"It should only be a couple more days."

"And then what? I have to sit there and wonder when the police are going to knock on the door? Or when somebody knocks on the door trying to sell something, I'll jump, thinking the police finally caught on to you? I don't want to live like that."

"And you won't have to."

"You're sure about that?" Stacy asked.

"Yes."

"They're already on to you."

"What?"

"The police were here a couple days ago, asking questions about you."

"What? Who was it?"

"I don't know. A couple of detectives. Lieutenant something or other, I don't remember their names."

As soon as she said lieutenant, Jack knew who it was. "What'd they want?"

"Asking questions about you. Said they knew you used to be part of Dom's crew and that you were seen at a restaurant with them."

"Yeah, he showed up there too," Jack said.

"He suspects you're doing something."

"He's just guessing. He doesn't have any proof. Just a lot of guesses. Did you tell him anything?"

"Of course not. I don't like or agree with what you're doing, but I would never say anything that would put you in more danger or jeopardize you in any way."

"Good."

"They asked if I knew what you were doing at that restaurant with all of them if you weren't involved in anything."

"What'd you tell them?"

"I said they wanted you to come back to the group,

but you were only at the restaurant as a courtesy, and that you were telling them no. That you couldn't come back."

"That's good."

"I guess it was more me wishing what I hoped you were going to say."

"It'll all be over soon," Jack said. "Only a few more days."

"Don't tell me specifics. I don't want to know anything. That way if the police show up again, I don't have to lie to them. Plus, it'll be easier if I don't know what time everything's supposed to happen. If I do, I'll probably be constantly looking at the clock and worrying."

"I'll call you when everything's over, OK? Will you come home then?"

"I don't know," Stacy replied. "I'll think about it."

"I love you. You know that, right?"

"I know."

"I'm not doing this for me, or because I miss it, or because I get kicks out of it, or because I miss the old times, or anything like that. If money was good for us right now, I wouldn't even bother. I'm doing it for us, for our family, so we can have a better chance. That's all."

"I know."

Suddenly, there was a knock on the door. Carter went over to the window and looked out to see who it was. He was a little stunned to see it was the police.

"Is someone there?" Stacy asked. "I heard a knock on the door."

"Oh, it's nothing. Looks like someone just trying to sell something. I'm gonna hang up so I can try and get rid of them. I'll call you when everything's over, OK?"

"Yeah."

"I love you."

Stacy hesitated for a second, but couldn't deny saying it no matter what was happening. "I love you too."

Carter put hung up and put his phone in his pocket to open the door. He opened it, revealing Lieutenant Downing and Detective Gruber.

"Something I can do for you guys?" Carter asked.

"We were in the neighborhood," Downing replied. "Figured we'd stop in and say hi."

Carter smirked. "OK. Hi. We done now?"

"Let's have a small chat."

"Thought we already did that."

"That was with everyone else around. Sometimes in this business, people are afraid to talk freely and openly when there's other people around, you know, fearing the repercussions."

"Everything I told you at the restaurant was the truth."

"Mind if we come in?"

"What for?"

"Told you, just wanna chat."

"We can do that here."

"Why? What's the matter? Got something to hide in there?"

"Nope. Don't you guys need a search warrant to come in?"

"Not if you invite us," Downing answered. "Plus, we're not really looking for anything, and to be honest, I wouldn't expect to find anything if we were."

Carter sighed and stepped aside not really wanting to talk to them or let them in, but figured it would be better for him if he cooperated. "Come on in."

Downing and Gruber walked into the living room. They looked around, saw the kids' toys on the ground, family pictures on the wall, it was a little messy, but not unexpected for a family with kids. Not that Downing knew from personal experience since he had no kids of his own, but he suspected if he did, his place would look pretty similar.

"You guys want a drink or anything?" Carter asked, walking into the room and clearing off a few toys on the coffee table.

The detectives sat down on a brown microfiber sofa. "Nothing for me, thanks," Downing said. His partner said the same. "This is a pretty comfy couch."

"Yeah, it's nice. So, what do you guys want?"

"We've been doing some digging on you, Jack. You mind if I call you Jack?"

"That's my name."

"Anyway, like I said, we've been looking at you, and you know what we found?"

Carter shook his head, seeing one of their family pictures on the wall. "Can't imagine."

"You know what we found? Nothing. Nothing. We didn't find anything on you that would make us think this is a bad guy, or this is someone we need to keep an eye on, or this is someone who we need to get off the streets, nothing like that."

"So why are you here then?"

"You wanna know why we're here?" Downing asked. "Because I wanna keep it that way." Downing got up and started walking around the living room. "Look at these." He pointed to the numerous pictures on the wall and tables. "Look at these. This looks like a nice, happy family."

"Thanks."

Downing then pointed to the toys on the floor. "And these. Look at these. Toys. Kids. Happy little kids running around, playing. Everything about this place that I'm seeing screams happy environment. Doesn't it?"

"Yeah."

"Look at all this," Downing said, extending his arms out. "Nothing about this place says to me that you're a bad guy."

"'Cause I'm not."

"And I'd agree with that. But you do have a history."

"I've never been in jail," Carter replied.

"Yet, you continue to run around with your friends,

and if you're up to something, I will change that. I won't like it. I won't like it at all." Downing looked at the photos again. "I wouldn't want to break up this family. But I will if that's what you make me do."

"I'm not running around with anybody. All I did was have dinner with them."

"You in financial problems?"

Carter shrugged. "You know, we've had our share of problems like anybody else, but we're OK."

"I'm sure you're much better now that your old pal Dominic paid off your bills for you."

"I didn't ask him to do that."

"But guys like him don't do things like that without expecting something in return."

"He never asked for anything," Carter said.

"You ran around with that crew before, didn't you? It's in your file."

"I was young, didn't have anything. I made mistakes."

"The other three went to jail. You did not. You lucked out."

"I was fortunate."

"And you turned your life around, right?"

"That's right. Haven't done anything against the law since."

"With the help of Stacy, I'm sure," Downing said. "She's a beautiful woman. I can see how a woman like that could set a man straight."

"She is."

"Be a shame if you made her cry."

"I won't."

"We talked to her the other day you know."

"Oh? Anything interesting?" Carter asked.

"She loves you. That much is clear. What isn't clear is everything else. Your involvement, what the crew is planning, all of that."

"Can't help you with that."

"All that time at dinner and they didn't mention anything about what they were planning?"

"They did not. All we talked about was old-times, what we've been up to, things like that. If they're planning anything, I don't know anything about it. I'm not involved."

"For your sake, man, I hope you're leveling with us," Downing said. "Because you seem like a good guy. Got a nice family. I'd really hate to throw you in the bucket with the rest of those slobs." Carter didn't reply, but simply nodded. "We're watching them, keeping them close, so if they're up to something, we're gonna be on them, we're gonna be there. And they're gonna go down. Just make sure you don't go down with them."

"I won't."

Downing and Gruber then walked toward the door. They delivered their message loud and clear. Downing was hoping to put a little fear into Carter, in case he was involved, hoping he could steer him off that path if he was. The detectives opened the door and walked outside. Downing turned around to deliver something he hoped would stick in Carter's mind.

"Remember, they got nothing to lose. You do."

18

With only one more day to go before their job, Cirella called everyone together so they could go over the plans one more time. Once again, they met at the same restaurant as a few days ago. Though the main reason was to still go over the plans and solve any last-minute questions or problems, Cirella also wanted to make sure he was still the only one being followed. Even if the cops decided to follow all of them, it wouldn't have changed anything, it just would've altered his escape plans and made them a little more challenging.

Carter was the first one at the restaurant as Cirella had asked him to be. Though Cirella had the reputation as a bit of a hard-nose, he wasn't unsympathetic to Carter's issues. He knew it was unlikely that Carter would continue with the group long-term, so he didn't want to put the heat on him for only doing one job with them. As far as he was concerned, there was no need for the cops to even know Carter was with them again. As long as Cirella was the only one being followed, and the detectives didn't come in again, they wouldn't know Carter was there.

Carter was only waiting for a few minutes when Rollins and Brantly arrived. Cirella didn't show up until ten minutes after the others. He had a big white shopping bag that he put down under the table. After greeting everyone, and ordering some food, they got back down to business.

"What kept you?" Rollins asked.

"Took a little detour," Cirella replied. "Figured if they were gonna follow me, I should make them earn their money."

"Where'd you go?"

"Nowhere really. Drove for about two hours, stopping at various places, going inside, just sitting and waiting, making them think maybe I was up to something."

"Still that lieutenant on you?"

"Nah, looked like some other slugs. Any of you guys followed on the way here?" Cirella looked at them and each man shook his head. "You guys sure?"

"We all know how to spot a tail, Dom," Rollins answered. "We're good."

"All right."

"What about tomorrow?" Brantly asked. "How you gonna shake these guys for good?"

"I'm not gonna shake them for good," Cirella replied. "Just for a few hours."

"What do you mean?"

Cirella grabbed a napkin and started drawing on it. "I'm gonna drive to the mall and lose them there."

"The mall?" Rollins asked.

"Yeah. It's a huge place, three stories, thousands of people there, right?"

"Yeah."

Cirella pointed to an end-unit department store. "I'm gonna park right outside here and go in. You guys are already gonna be there, waiting in your car outside. If you see those detectives follow me in, I'm gonna go around and come out through here, one of the mall entrances. It's right next to the department store."

"And if they don't?" Rollins asked. "What if they just sit there and wait."

Cirella then drew a line across the mall, coming out on the other side. "Then you guys drive around to this side. It's where the mall buses park to drop off and pick up. It's a busy area, I can blend right in, then hop in the car and away we go."

"Then what?"

"Then we do the job," Cirella answered. "When the job's over, you guys drive me back to the mall and drop me off. Before leaving, I'll grab a few shirts to make it seem like I've been shopping the whole time. The whole thing shouldn't take more than two or three hours anyway."

"What about me?" Carter asked. "Where do I come in?"

"I want you at the mall too."

"Why?"

"Because you're gonna call out of work tomorrow, right?"

"Yeah."

"After the job's done, the cops are gonna investigate, and they might start with us," Cirella said. "You calling out of work and not having any kind of alibi, that's gonna stick out like a sore thumb. They might think you're involved somehow."

"OK?"

Cirella then pointed to the other end of the mall. "I want you to park here. About ten minutes before twelve, I want you to purchase something with your credit card, so there's proof you were there. You meet up with me at twelve at one of those two spots depending on what the detectives do. I'll be in contact with you after I get there."

"OK, sounds pretty good," Carter said.

"When we get back after the job, you purchase something else, then you leave. That way if they look at you, they can see you purchased something before and after the job was supposed to happen. You'll have the alibi of being at the mall shopping. They won't be able to prove you were anywhere else."

"What about cameras?" Rollins asked. "They got

cameras at the mall. The cops will check them, and they'll see you guys moving in and out."

Cirella smiled, knowing he had that covered too. He reached underneath the table and pulled out a couple of jackets. He handed one to Carter.

"What's this?" Carter asked.

"Reversible jackets. We wear one side going in, the other side going out." Cirella also pulled out a couple of baseball hats. He handed one to Carter. "Tape this to the inside of your jacket on the way in. Then put it on before you leave. That way they see our faces going in, but on the way out, we got on different jackets and hats; they won't be able to make us out."

Carter put the hat on to try it out. "Then on the way out after the job's been pulled, we reverse the jackets back to the original side we wore on the way in, ditch the hats, and we're good."

"Exactly. What do you guys think? Sound like a plan?"

Everyone nodded. "Sounds good," Rollins said.

"I like it," Brantly replied.

"It should work," Carter said.

"What about you two?" Cirella asked. "What'd you guys come up with?"

"I gave my credit card to my sister," Rollins said. "Told her to use it at exactly two o'clock downtown at one of those automatic car washes. No cameras there or nothing."

"Good. What about you?"

"Gave my parents my card," Brantly replied. "Told them to visit one of those independent bookstores and charge a few things."

"Any cameras in there?"

"No, it's clean."

"You're sure?"

"Yeah, I've been in there. It's good."

"Good," Cirella said. "So everyone's got a record of being somewhere else when this job goes down."

Rollins smirked. "We're gonna pull this job off right under their noses, just like you said."

"I told you it'd work."

"What about the money?" Carter asked. "Any idea the final tally yet?"

"Not yet," Cirella replied. "Mark thinks it's gonna be in the neighborhood of 1.2, maybe 1.4 million."

"What's the final cut?" Rollins wondered.

"We're each probably gonna get around a hundred fifty."

"That only works out to around six hundred thousand. Where's the rest going?"

"Mark's gotta take care of the rest," Cirella answered. "Hundred thousand goes to the guys blocking traffic. Mark gets his cut. Then there's I think two more guys who gave him the inside info about the job. They get full shares as well."

Rollins quickly added the numbers up in his head. "That takes it up to... what, 1.1, something like that?"

"Yeah," Cirella said with a shrug, not concerned

about it. "If there's an extra couple grand, it'll get split up as well. Don't get caught up over pennies. A hundred and fifty gees is a good take for all of us. If it gets bumped up to one seventy-five, two hundred, so be it. But one fifty's the base. Not a bad haul."

The group nodded.

"But remember," Cirella said. "You can't spend or save the money if you're dead or locked up. Each of us has to make sure we play it right tomorrow. All the way down the line. We do that, we'll be in the clear. If we don't... there'll be bad times ahead."

19

Carter woke up early, just after six, and stared up at the ceiling. His heart was beating heavily just thinking about what he was going to do today. He was up late last night too, having a hard time falling asleep as all the possible scenarios ran through his mind. Some of them good, some of them bad. He probably didn't get more than four hours of sleep.

Back when he was running with the crew for a living, he never had a problem sleeping. It was just business as usual, no big deal. But now, he was a different man. He had a family, he had a job, a house, he had everything to lose. Back then, he had nothing to lose, including his life. That's how they all thought at the time. Now he was older, and hopefully wiser. It used to be about making money, doing jobs for the thrill of it. Now it was only about supporting his family.

Carter's hands were clammy and his mouth was dry. He'd already called out from work the night before, saying that he wasn't feeling well. He never called out so he wasn't given any flak for it unlike some guys who seemed to call out every week. But it would turn out to be a slow morning for him. It seemed as though time was standing still, taking forever to get to the point where he needed to leave.

When the time reached eleven thirty, Carter looked at the picture of his family sitting on an end table. He reached down and picked it up, smiling at them. He then brought the picture up to his lips and kissed it, hoping everything went according to plan so he could have them in his arms again. He put his hand on the picture, then put it back down on the table and headed for the door. As he walked outside, he called Cirella to let him know he was on the way.

"Hey, just wanted to let you know I'm leaving now."

"Good," Cirella replied. "Any cops outside your place?"

"No, nothing."

"You sure?"

Carter went to the end of the driveway and looked up and down the street. He didn't see any cars that were occupied, and none that weren't familiar to him. Every car that was parked on the street were the same ones he'd been seeing since they moved in two years ago.

"Yeah, it's all good," Carter said. "No unfamiliar vehicles here."

"Good. You start heading to the mall now. Do what we talked about. You good with that?"

"Yeah, no problem."

"All right," Cirella said. "I'll be leaving in a few minutes so we should probably get there around the same time. You need to go over anything again?"

"No, I'm good."

"All right, I'll call you when I get there. See you in a bit."

As soon as he was done with Carter, Cirella called his other friends to make sure they were on the same path.

"Hey, where you guys at?" Cirella asked.

"We're sitting outside the mall right now," Rollins answered.

"Got everything?"

"We're ready to roll. Got the truck, got our gear, only thing missing is you guys."

"Anything left to do?"

"No, we switched the plates already. We got a Maryland plate on it now."

"Good. Have to lose anybody?"

"No, piece of cake. It's like they're not even trying."

"Well, having a shortage of manpower's probably got a lot to do with that," Cirella said. "Plus, they don't have any idea what we're up to. If they did, I'm sure they'd be tailing all of us right now."

"What about you? Still got someone sitting there?"

Cirella went over to his window and looked between the blinds, looking down at the parking lot. He saw the same unmarked vehicle that had now become pretty familiar to him, complete with two detectives sitting inside.

"Yeah, they're still here," Cirella said. "Jack's already on his way so I'm gonna start moving in a minute or two."

"We'll be ready."

Cirella grabbed his jacket and left his apartment. After exiting the building, he walked toward his car. Along the way, he looked at the detectives who were still keeping an eye on him and gave them a wave. The detectives didn't seem pleased at his sense of humor.

"Prick," one of the detectives said.

"I really hope this guy does something stupid so we can take him in," the other one replied.

"I hear ya. I'm getting pretty tired of sitting on him. If these guys don't do something soon, we're gonna have to start working something else. Can't sit on them forever."

"We really shouldn't even be sitting on them now. I mean, we don't have any concrete information that they're doing or planning anything. This is just on Downing's hunch."

"Yeah, but his hunches are usually pretty good."

"I know, but I have a feeling he's off on this one."

"We'll see."

The detective in the passenger seat tapped his partner, seeing Cirella's car pull out. "He's moving."

The detectives followed Cirella out of the complex, staying relatively close to him. Cirella kept an eye on them through his rearview mirror the entire time. For once, he didn't want to lose them. He was making sure he was driving at a normal pace so they could keep up. It took about twenty minutes until they got to the mall. Cirella pulled in front of the department store, just like he planned. Before getting out of the car, he noticed the black SUV of theirs parked two lanes away. Cirella put his ear comm in.

"You guys read me?"

"Loud and clear," Rollins replied.

"Jack, you here?"

"Yeah, I just bought a shirt," Carter answered. "Heading to the mall part now."

"Good. You know where to meet me. I'll be there in five."

"Roger."

Cirella got out of the car and stretched his arms, casually looking around to see where the detectives were. He didn't see them at first glance.

"You guys see the cops?" Cirella asked.

"About five rows behind you," Rollins said. "They parked in between a bunch of cars to try to blend in. You're good to go."

Cirella walked into the department store. Rollins and Brantly stayed put for a minute to see how the detectives would react. One of them got out of the car and followed Cirella in while the other stayed in the car.

"Dom, you got one coming in," Rollins said.

"All right. You guys drive around to the other side."

"On the move."

Cirella walked into the men's clothing department, then dropped down to one knee, making sure he wasn't in sight of any store cameras. He grabbed his baseball hat and put it on, then took off his jacket and reversed it. He put sunglasses on and tugged his hat down to try to conceal his face as much as possible. He took a look around to see if he could spot the detective following him, but he didn't notice him. With the plan going according to schedule, Cirella walked into the mall, making a beeline for the exit he was supposed to meet Carter at. After a few minutes, he saw Carter standing there by the glass doors, his back against the wall.

"You reverse that?" Cirella asked.

"Yeah."

Cirella patted him on the shoulder. "Good. You guys out there?"

"We're here," Rollins answered. "Come out, we're three rows to your right, about twelve spots down."

Cirella tapped Carter on the arm. "Let's go."

The two men walked out of the mall, their heads

tucked down to avoid being seen by cameras, then followed Rollins' instructions to find the car. Cirella and Carter both hopped in the back seat so they could get changed again. They each had a bag at their respective seats with new clothes for them to change into. Rollins and Brantly were already in their black outfits.

"What about the semi?" Cirella asked after he'd finished changing.

"It's already parked at the spot," Brantly answered.

"You're sure?"

"Damn well better be. Just put it there two hours ago."

"Any problems getting it?"

"No. That guy Mark set us up with was easy. No sweat."

"Nice. All right, we'll head there first to drop Isaac off. Then the rest of us will go further down the road to wait for the armored car."

"Any chance the cops are on to this?" Rollins asked.

"Only if one of you knuckleheads told them."

"Fat chance of that."

"Don't worry about it. We're good. Only thing we have to worry about is some random police patrol car that happens to be there at the time. Other than that, should be gravy."

"Where are we gonna wait?"

"I dunno. There's a couple spots down that street

that we could set up in. Depends on traffic and if people are already parked there or not."

"What if we just follow the armored car from their last pickup spot?"

"No, I don't wanna do that," Cirella replied. "We follow them the whole way they might start getting nervous. I don't want them to have any clue what's coming for them."

Cirella glanced over at Carter, who was looking a little nervous. Carter had that bewildered look on his face, the kind someone gets when they feel like they don't know what they're doing.

"You all right?" Cirella asked.

Carter snapped out of his trance. "Yeah. Yeah, I'm good."

"Be just like old times."

"Yeah."

Carter started nodding, trying to make himself believe it. It wasn't like old times though. Not even close. Carter was out of his element now and he knew it. This wasn't his life anymore. He had a gun in his hands, they were about to knock over an armored car, bullets could be flying, there was nothing about this job that he was comfortable with. When he agreed to this, he thought it would come back to him. That it would be no big deal. He figured he would still have nerves of steel, like he used to have, that they could pull the job off with no problem. But here he was. His stomach was tied up in knots. He was as nervous now

as he was the day his first child was born. The uncertainty of what was to come was almost too much. He
knew there was no backing out now. He just had to grit
his teeth and hope that he could do what was expected
of him. He didn't want to let anyone down, including
himself. Carter closed his eyes for a moment and
thought of his family. He hoped he was making the
right choice. He had to hope he would make his way
through this unscathed.

20

The team drove down County Road, the street all the action was going to happen on. They saw two men in construction outfits, hard hats, bright orange vests, beginning to block off the road. They had a van and started to put orange cones along the road to prevent anyone from driving down. One of the men came up to the SUV to try to direct them somewhere else.

"Hey buddy, they're about to start tearing up the road down here, you gotta use a different road."

"Mark sends his regards," Cirella said.

"Oh, you're the guys?"

"Yep."

"All right, we'll let you through."

"Just make sure you don't let anyone else in."

"No worries, man, we got it."

The crew drove through once a few of the cones

were moved. It only took a few minutes to get to the semi that Brantly had parked along the backroad earlier that morning. Once they got there, Brantly grabbed his black bag and hopped out of the car.

"You got everything?" Cirella asked.

Brantly looked in his bag to make sure his weapons were there even though he already knew they were. "Yeah, I'm good."

"I'll let you know when we're on the way. You know what to do after that."

"Yep. As soon as I see that armored car, I'm revving the semi up, then I'm gonna light that car up."

"All right. If anything looks fishy or out of whack, let us know."

"Will do."

Cirella was initially going to have Carter drive, that way he and Rollins could quickly jump out of the passenger seats, but judging by the looks of him, he wasn't sure Carter could handle it. Though he didn't look quite as nervous, Cirella needed to know whoever was behind the wheel, they weren't going to panic. So he had Rollins get in the driver's seat. As they drove down the road, Cirella looked at his watch.

"They should have left their last stop about two minutes ago. We should be seeing them in about fifteen minutes."

Once they got to the next intersection, they saw the other two men starting to set up as well. Dressed in the same hard hats and orange vests, they started lining up the cones, though they weren't blocking the street off yet. As they drove up to the men, Cirella rolled down his window and stuck his head out. One of the workers came up to him.

"You guys ready?" Cirella asked.

"You guys the crew who's doing this?"

"Yeah. Any questions?"

"Nope. We got this. We're gonna let the armored car through, then you guys, then that's it."

"All right. They should get here in about fifteen minutes."

"We're ready."

Rollins drove up and down the street for a few more minutes, trying to find the best place to sit and wait. They eventually settled on a paved area in front of a trucking business. They were off the street and out of the way if any trucks drove into the facility.

"I hope there's no cars already on its tail," Rollins said. "That'll make it more difficult to get in behind it."

"We'll worry about that if it happens," Cirella replied.

They sat there for the next ten minutes, anxiously waiting for their first view of the armored car. They each got out their automatic rifles and checked them as well as the backup pistols they always carried on them. Carter cleared his throat and looked down between his legs. He started swaying his knees back and forth out of sheer nervousness. Cirella and Rollins both looked back at him and could see how distressed he was. Cirella and Rollins then glanced at each other, Rollins giving him a look that indicated he was concerned. Cirella put his hand up to try to ease his fears. He believed that Carter would be fine once it was go-time.

"You all right, Jack?" Cirella asked.

"Yeah, I'm good."

"Just like riding a bike, buddy. You don't ride for a few years, you don't forget how to push the pedals. Just gotta get back on and go. You'll get to where you wanna end up."

Carter whispered to himself. "Just hope I don't stumble before I get there."

Five more minutes went by. Then they saw it.

"There it is," Rollins said.

They stayed in their spot until the armored car drove by.

"Let's roll," Cirella said.

Since there were no other cars immediately in the vicinity, Rollins was able to pull in right behind their target with no issues. They drove steady down the road until finally stopping at the roadblock. They waited for about a minute.

"Hope these guys know what they're doing," Rollins said.

"They'll be fine," Cirella replied. "Just focus on what we need to do. Everything else will take care of itself."

The armored car started moving with Rollins

moving right behind them. After they went through, both Cirella and Rollins looked in the mirror to make sure the road was getting blocked again behind them. It was.

"Remember to give them some room," Cirella said. "Isaac's gonna ram it, so we don't need to be that close."

"What if he misses?" Rollins asked.

"He won't miss. He worked out the calculations, he did a few practice runs, he's good. You know he won't screw this up."

Rollins let up on the gas, giving plenty of distance between them and the armored car.

"Isaac, you're up," Cirella said. "You got about a minute."

They could already hear the engine of the semi running. He even blew the horn. "All ready over here. That's a ten-four, good buddy."

All three of the men in the SUV let out a laugh. "What are you, a trucker now or something?"

"Just wanted to get in the mood."

"Keep your eyes open. You're up in less than a minute."

"I'm ready, Freddy."

Carter finally had a smile on his face, appreciating the humor. It seemed to calm him down a little. Rollins had slowed up so much that the armored car was almost out of sight. With the target being closer to Brantly now, Rollins sped up, not wanting to get there too long after the crash. It needed to be timed perfectly so that the guards didn't have a chance to get situated after the crash.

The armored car came around the small bend, now in sight of Brantly. "Here we go!"

Brantly waited about five more seconds before putting the semi in drive. He put it into full gear as the car approached. He'd practiced this run several times in the past few days, and he used a visual marker of a tree, so that when the car passed that tree, that's when he put the semi in motion. He was going full blast by the time the car got to his location. There were trees on both sides of the unpaved road, partially hiding him so the armored car couldn't see him coming. As the car got to his location, Brantly blasted out of hiding, smacking the armored car right in the side. A thunderous smack and crackle could be heard as the two heavy trucks collided. The armored car turned over onto its side. Just as the car flipped over, the SUV carrying the other members of the crew came speeding over.

All four members of the crew jumped out of their vehicles. With their black masks on, Cirella and Brantly went over to the front of the car to cover the driver and the other guard. Carter stood in the middle of the road, constantly looking in every direction for signs of trouble. Rollins went over to the back of the car and planted an explosive on the door. With the driver and passenger not moving, Cirella moved to the back of the car with Rollins.

Cirella and Rollins then took cover next to the car itself. Within a few seconds, a loud explosion rattled the area, blowing the doors completely off the car. As smoke filled the car, Cirella and Rollins came back around, their guns extended fully, pointing at the occupants. There were two guards back there. They were both moving around. One was lying on the floor, stunned by what just happened. The other had gotten back to his feet and was reaching for his gun. Cirella quickly tried to persuade him not to do something stupid.

"No, no, no, no! You don't wanna do that." The man stood there, staring at the men, still contemplating what he wanted to do. "Trust me, you don't wanna do something you'll regret. The money's not yours, don't lose your life over twelve dollars an hour. Come out, put your hands up, and as soon as we're done, I give you my word you guys will still be alive to go home to your wives, girlfriends, and kids. Don't make me do something I don't wanna do."

The man knew he had no choice but to hope these thieves were of their word. He put the gun down and put his hands up, slowly walking out of the car. The other guard got back to his feet and did the same. Rollins put them both on the ground, lying face first with their arms stretched out to their side. He motioned to Carter to come over and watch them. They tried not to speak when possible to avoid the witnesses hearing their voices, and they didn't use names at all so they couldn't be identified. Brantly kept watch over the drivers, both of whom started stirring.

With the dangerous parts out of the way, Cirella and Rollins went inside the car and started removing its contents. There were boxes and bags filled with money, checks, jewelry, even gold. A few minutes went by and the passenger guard started moving around more freely.

"Hands up!" Brantly said, pointing his rifle directly at him. The guard wasn't complying. "Don't be stupid!"

Cirella heard the commotion and tapped Rollins on the arm to go over and help out. They were just about finished cleaning out the car, and he didn't want anyone to get hurt at this point. Having to face a murder rap on top of the robbery would just be silly. There was nothing left for the guards to guard. As Cirella continued carrying items from the car to the SUV, Rollins went over to the front and also pointed his gun at the man.

"Hey," Rollins said, just wanting to make sure the guard knew he was there also.

Upon seeing both men there, the guard tossed his gun away and put his hands up, climbing out of the vehicle. He stood there for a minute as the driver also came to, following him out of the car. Brantly directed both unarmed men to the ground, laying them face down next to the others. With Carter watching them, Rollins and Brantly joined Cirella in emptying out the car. It only took another minute. Carter continued watching the men as the other three got into the SUV.

"Let's go!" Cirella yelled at him.

Carter ran over and jumped into the car, Rollins immediately taking off. The men took off their masks as they sped on down the road.

"Semi's clean, right?" Cirella asked.

"Wore gloves, no prints," Brantly answered.

"Good."

"Wooooo," Rollins yelled in excitement. "Came off smooth as butter."

"We're not out of the woods yet," Cirella said. "Let's make sure there's no issues at the roadblock."

There was nothing to worry about though. Once they got to the roadblock, it was quiet as could be. They gave the two workers there a thumbs up to let them know it went off without a hitch. After letting the crew out, the workers got back in their van and drove off, leaving the cones to block the road so nobody would stumble upon the armored car for a bit.

"Back to the mall?" Rollins asked.

"Ehh, let's go to the storage unit first," Cirella replied. "I don't really like driving around with all this cash and stuff. You still got your cars there, right?"

"Yeah."

"Let's do that then."

Brantly was looking through a few of the bags. "Looks like a lot of bread here."

Cirella looked back at him. "Remember, we're not

gonna be able to use that right away. The cops will be looking for it. They'll be checking our bank accounts for large deposits. We gotta play it cool."

"How long?" Carter asked.

"Might be a few months. Mark's gonna have to work his magic, sell the non-cash items, turn the bad cash that's marked into good cash that's not. It'll take some time. It works out in our favor though."

"How you figure?"

"Because the cops are gonna look to us first. If we don't have anything, if we got nothing to spend, eventually they'll move on. This way we won't be tempted for a while. It works out better for us. We'll be good."

21

The crew went back to the storage unit to park the car, change clothes, and then take Cirella and Carter back to the mall. To try to make it even more difficult for the police to put things together, they travelled back in separate cars. Rollins took Cirella while Brantly took Carter. That way, even if they suspected the pair left the mall together, they'd come back separately, and in different vehicles, making IDing them all the more difficult.

Cirella stopped and bought a shirt on the way out of the department store. As he walked back to his car, he looked over at the spot the detectives were, and the car was still sitting there. He noticed two outlines in the front seat, so he knew they were there. Cirella looked at his watch. It was exactly two hours from when he first arrived at the mall. They timed everything perfectly. As he got in his car, he checked in with the others.

"Jack, you good?"

"Getting in my car now," Carter answered.

"What about you other guys?"

"I'm good," Rollins said.

"Me too," Brantly replied. "I'm gonna go meet up with my family, that way if the cops come asking, people will remember I was there."

"Good idea," Cirella said. "I'll check in with you guys later."

Cirella drove straight home, still with the police following him, though he really didn't care anymore. They pulled the job off. He knew the cops couldn't touch them. Even if they suspected it, they couldn't prove it. It would be more difficult to get the things to Mark to spin off if the police stayed on his tail, but if necessary, he could just have Rollins and Brantly meet Mark at the storage unit to pass it off.

As Carter was driving home, he called Stacy. He didn't want to wait until he got home. He wanted to let her know that it was done and over with, with the hope that she would finally come home again. Much to his surprise, she picked up on the first ring.

"Hey, glad you picked up so fast."

It was unusual for him to call her in the middle of the day unless it was something really important. "Where are you?" Stacy asked. "Are you at work?"

"No, I called out today."

"Is today the... the thing you're doing?"

"It's over," Jack said. "It's done."

"Really?"

"Yeah. I'm driving home now. Everything worked out fine, no problems, just like I said."

"I don't care about the money or any of that. I just want to know that you're safe."

"I am," Jack replied. "It's all good. Everything was perfect. It might be a few months before I get my share of the money because we have to make sure the police aren't tracing it or anything, but it should be close to a hundred and fifty thousand."

"Like I said, I don't care about the money. My only concern is keeping this family together."

"We are. At least we will be when you come home."

"I'm already home," Stacy said.

"You are?"

"I came back about an hour ago. I didn't want to be away from you anymore."

"And the kids?"

"The kids are here too."

"You guys are what I live for."

"Promise me this is it," Stacy said. "No more jobs, no more anything. I don't want to live like that, and I don't want to put our kids through it."

"I promise you this was the last time. If they ask again, I'm out. I give you my word. Even if they say it's an easy job, I'm done. We should be able to live comfortably from here on out. I don't want to risk losing you."

"What about the police?"

"It shouldn't be an issue."

"You're sure?"

"Pretty sure. There's nothing for them to latch onto. I promise."

"OK. Hurry up and get home, OK? The kids miss you."

"I'll be right there."

ONCE CIRELLA GOT BACK to his apartment, he called Mark to let him know how the job went and discuss further details.

"How'd it go?" Mark asked.

"Piece of cake. Everything went off without a hitch."

"Perfect. Where's the stuff?"

"It's at one of our storage units."

"How soon can you get it to me?"

"Hopefully within a few days," Cirella answered. "Wanna see if this tail pulls off me permanently first. If not, I'll have the boys bring it to you. I don't wanna keep shaking them and make them think something's up."

"No, that's fine."

"How soon you think we'll get our cut?"

"Why, you hurting for money?"

"No, just so I can give the boys a general time frame."

"I'm thinking about three months," Mark said. "If any of you need a little something to hold you over until then, just hit me up."

"Should be fine."

The pair hung up a few minutes later, leading Cirella to relax for a little while. He put an old gangster movie on. About an hour later, he got another call. It was Mark. Cirella knew something was up.

"Sorry to call you again so soon, but I figured I'd give you a heads up."

"What's going on?" Cirella asked.

"Just heard from my contact down at the police building."

"Yeah?"

"Downing's headed for you right now."

"What for?"

"Think he wants to question you."

"He doesn't have an arrest warrant with him, does he?"

"No, just wants to talk from what I understand," Mark said.

"That's all right. Let him. I can handle him."

"All right. Just wanted to let you know what you're in store for."

"How much time?"

"Probably within the hour."

"Thanks."

Cirella looked out the window for the next little while, anxiously waiting for his visitor to arrive. Mark was right about the time. Downing got to the apartment about forty-five minutes after Mark called. Cirella went to the door in anticipation of his adversary knocking. Once the detective knocked, Cirella answered right away.

Downing grinned as the door opened. "Quick. Almost like you knew we were coming."

"Saw you out the window."

"Can we come in?"

Cirella held his arm out. "Sure. You wanna search the place?"

"You're always so quick to offer."

"That's 'cause I got nothing to hide."

Cirella closed the door once his company was inside. "You boys want a soda or iced tea or something?"

"We're good, thanks."

"So, what can I help you with?" Cirella asked.

"We had something go down a couple hours ago. An armored car got hit."

"Oh yeah? What was the damage?"

"Probably over a million."

Cirella nodded. "Pretty good take."

"You don't happen to know anything about that, do you?"

"'Fraid not, boys. Been here all day. Except I did run out to the mall for about two hours."

"Yeah, we know," Downing said. "Just so happens that's when the car got hit. Right in that time frame."

"No kidding? Coincidence."

"I'm sure."

"You got a suspect yet?"

"I'm looking at a crew."

"Well, I hope you get them."

"I will," Downing replied.

"Hopefully they're not too smart for you."

"About the mall, can you prove you were there?"

"Didn't your boys follow me there?"

"Then they lost you."

"That's a tough break for me," Cirella said. "Oh, wait, I got something." Cirella walked over to his shopping bag and reached inside, taking out a receipt. He brought it over to Downing and handed it to him. "There you go."

"What's this?"

"I bought a shirt while I was there."

Downing, with an unpleasant look on his face, glanced at Gruber, thinking they were being outsmarted. He had a feeling Cirella's crew was good for this, but he didn't have proof. Just a feeling.

"What time did you say this job went down?" Cirella asked.

"Let's say a little before one."

"That's too bad for you. I got to the mall about

twelve. Looked around for a while. Didn't see a whole lot to my liking, except for that shirt which I bought around one thirty or so. Guess that's what gives me what you call an alibi, huh?"

"I can dig around to see if I can shoot some holes in that alibi," Downing said.

"Go ahead. Doesn't worry me. Know why? 'Cause I wasn't there. I know you've been following me around this past week figuring me and my boys were about to hit something, but we didn't do this job."

"I'm gonna keep digging. I'll get to the bottom of this."

"I'm sure you will. You let me know if you find anything, huh?"

"You'll be the first to know."

"How much longer you gonna keep that tail on me?"

"Why, need to pawn stuff off?"

Cirella smiled. "Listen, we both know you can't keep that on me forever, especially if you ain't got nothing on me. You're gonna eventually get told by your superiors to pull them off me and work on something else. So even if I was good for this job, I ain't got money burning a hole in my pocket. I can wait longer than you can."

"Is that an admission?"

Cirella laughed. "C'mon, get real. We both know you're on a fishing expedition here."

"Maybe. Sometimes you get a big fish that way."

"Yeah, and sometimes you get a big bag of nothing. You got nothing, you're not gonna find nothing, so if you wanna keep digging, go ahead."

"You're not worried in the slightest, are you?"

"Not at all."

They went back and forth for several more minutes before Downing decided to leave, knowing he wasn't going to get anywhere. As the detectives exited the apartment, Downing turned around to give some lasting advice.

"Keep that halo on tight, huh? I'd hate to see it come crashing down."

"No worries. I'm not getting tripped up by it."

"Well, enjoy the rest of your day, huh?"

"Oh, I will. Beautiful day so far, isn't it?"

"I'm sure we'll be seeing each other again."

"I wouldn't count on it."

ABOUT THE AUTHOR

Mike Ryan is the popular author of The Silencer Series, The Cain Series, The Eliminator Series, and The Ghost Series, along with several standalone titles. He lives in Pennsylvania with his wife and four children, and three dogs. He's always hard at work on another book. Visit his website at www.mikeryanbooks.com to sign up for his newsletter, as well as vote on reader polls.

ALSO BY MIKE RYAN

The Silencer Series

The Eliminator Series

The Cain Series

The Ghost Series

A Dangerous Man

The Last Job